ALSO BY HY BRETT

NONFICTION
THE ULTIMATE NEW YORK CITY TRIVIA

A BOOK OF LOVE FOR MY SON
(With H. Jackson Brown)

HUMOR
WISHFUL WEDDINGS
*From Casablanca to Titanic...Star Crossed Lovers
United at Last!*

A SECRET REPORT TO THE TRUE AMERICAN
FAITH SOCIETY
Senior Citizens and Their Threat to America

HOW TO SURVIVE THE NEW MILLENNIUM
Recycled Wisdom for an Age of Diminished Expectations

MYSTERY
PROMISES TO KEEP
(With Barbara Brett)

THE HITMAN OF AVENUE U

Hy Brett

THE HITMAN OF AVENUE U by Hy Brett

Cover design by Barbara Rainess

Author services by Pedernales Publishing, LLC.
www.pedernalespublishing.com

Library of Congress Control Number: 2018943591

ISBN: Paperback edition 978-0-9979710-2-6
ISBN: Digital edition 978-0-9979710-3-3

Printed in the United States of America

For Barbara
My wife and the big hit of my life

Wednesday, February 11, 1981

M Y HEART POUNDED as I put the Smith and Wesson .38 into my canvas portfolio. It said, *Sunshine Tours 1979,* and showed a hula dancer in front of a huge orange sun. The portfolio had been a gift from Jane Fairlie, the travel editor of the *New York Globe,* where I was once a mail clerk. Early in 1981, she was killed and robbed during her annual VIP junket to Jamaica, often described in her popular Sunday column as "my island paradise."

"That's a nice weapon you've selected," Mr. Anthony said. He flashed all of his large white teeth, and brushed a speck from the lapel of his black cashmere jacket. Then he snapped a gold Tiffany lighter to the Marlboro Light that might save him from lung cancer but not from a bullet from a Mafioso whom he had disrespected, even without intention. Never had I been so close to a gentleman with more class. According to Big Nick, who was going to be my *patròno* in the organization, Mr. Anthony's hairpiece was by a Frenchie whose clientele included movie stars, TV anchors and U.S. senators. Three Republicans and two Democrats, to be exact. "What the fuck?" Big Nick had said about the senators. "They may not give a shit about us average voters who pay for their salaries and perks, but they certainly know how to take care of themselves. Am I right or am I wrong?"

We were in the Plaza Hotel on Fifth Avenue, and Mr. Anthony's lighter, rings, watch and cuff links looked very appropriate in the elegant room overlooking Central Park. On a clear day I could probably have seen more of the Upper West Side and the handiwork of a few of Big Nick's associates who specialized in arson, just as doctors may specialize in cancer and lawyers in hiding money overseas. He had told me that they were scheduled today to torch a rental property for a developer who had contributed *mucho* to politicians but could wait no longer for them to end rent control and rent stabilization. These programs for the poor, which were alien to such American values as self-reliance, were depriving the developer of his ambition to become as rich and powerful as Donald Trump, his role model and also the future president of the United States, or so Trump liked to brag to close pals at the ultra-exclusive Le Club in the East Fifties.

Big Nick Lombardi had sent me to the Plaza to get my personal gun from Mr. Anthony, his source for clean equipment that the cops and Feds couldn't trace in a million years. When I expressed surprise at this elaborate procedure for a simple handgun and not, for example, the famous cannon from Fort Hamilton in Brooklyn, Big Nick was kind enough to explain it to me:

"Believe me, George, it's worth the extra few bucks. You get what you pay for in this fucken world, and it'll probably be the same in the next world too, which is why I contribute not only to Catholic charities but to quite a few Jewish ones, including a kosher nursing home in the Bronx where the chicken cacciatore ain't at all bad, or so I've heard from Father Marco, who attends an interfaith dinner there from time to time. Their kosher wine is nothing to speak of, however. Look, if you wanted a first-class lay, you wouldn't go to one of those ancient whores who hang out in Tony's bar, would you? The last time one of them had a period was probably back in the Dark Ages. Am I right or am I wrong?"

"You're right a hundred percent," I had said at once, because you didn't dare say anything else to a man who controls so much of the action in town and refers to politicians and judges as Mickey and Benny.

It had taken me a long time to make up my mind to join up with Big Nick, not that I didn't appreciate the honor of being invited into his family. Born in the Gravesend part of Brooklyn, we had been each other's best pal all through St. Edmund's Elementary, Cunningham Junior High, and finally James Madison High. In those distant days, long before his Uncle Vito became capo and took him under his wing, I had been the powerful one, and I used to protect Nick from bullies who preyed on him because he was short and fat and wore thick eyeglasses like Mr. Magoo in the old cartoons on TV. Unlike people I was to meet later on in life, he remembered and appreciated past favors. Last night, after arranging for my visit to Mr. Anthony at the Plaza, he had once again quoted from Dale Carnegie, one of his mentors and favorite authors: "'I honestly believe this is one of the great secrets to true peace of mind—a decent set of values.'"

Mr. Anthony cleared his throat as if he were coughing up a fishbone in polite company at a Holy Name dinner right here at the Plaza Hotel. "If you don't mind my saying so," he said, "you don't look at all like the usual sort of zapper in Big Nick's family."

I was not sure whether he meant his remark as a compliment or a criticism. If as a criticism, he could have been referring to my age, fifty, and to my graying hair, the result of a serious disposition all my life, and worse than ever in recent months because of my unemployment and dwindling bank account. Or maybe I just didn't look to him like a guy who could pull the trigger of a gun, the deed that, like surviving the famous full-hour specialty of Bubbles Bernstein at the Capri Recreation Center, separated the boys from the men. Maybe I just wasn't a killer.

Reading my thoughts, Big Nick had assured me last night that he didn't have me in mind just yet for a triggerman, but he said it would be useful for me to have the gun and to feel at home with it, "like a medical student with his stethoscope." He had offered me another quote from Dale Carnegie: "'We may not think we can, but we have surprisingly strong inner resources that will see us through if we will only make use of them. We are stronger than we think!'"

Mr. Anthony said to me, "You don't talk much, do you?"

"Sorry. I was just thinking about this, that, and the other thing, you know."

"There's certainly a lot to think about in this fucken life. Why are we here? And what's the meaning of it all? Why was Donald Trump, who owns at least a hundred properties, born to a real estate millionaire while I myself was born to a mere waiter in a spaghetti joint in Sheepshead Bay? Luckily, poor Pop was hit pretty bad by a pizza delivery truck and was able to collect a tidy sum thanks to our priest, Father Leo, and his interfaith contact with Loophole Louie Levine, a shyster affiliated with our local Democratic Club on Coney Island Avenue. One of these days I'm going to drop out of the loop and go into retreat in a monastery, taking along only a loaf of bread, a salami and maybe a redhead with a big ass and tits. Big Nick once said he could arrange it with a certain bishop in Jersey."

"The redhead too?"

"Why not? As it must have been written somewhere,

'Man does not live by bread and salami alone.'" He winked.

"I guess you're right. You name it and I'm sure Big Nick can do it. I've never seen anyone with more clout and charisma."

Earlier, Mr. Anthony had spread out about two dozen guns on the bed for my examination, and now he began to pack them into the compartments of a leather suitcase such as I had seen displayed in the windows of the finest shops on Madison Avenue. When he looked in pain suddenly, I offered him a couple of my extra-strength Tums, but he shook his head and made a weak smile.

"Thanks, pal," he said. "I'm afraid it ain't heartburn but an affair of the heart, as Dear Abby would say. There are two gorgeous broads I can take to dinner and screw tonight, and I can't decide between them."

"I wish *I* had such problems," I said, in order to be polite. And also to prove I wasn't gay, which was as big a no-no as an Italian wife's using ketchup, even Heinz, as the sauce for her meatballs and spaghetti.

"Believe you me, it can certainly be a problem. They keep telling me how horny they are, and my natural inclination as a good Christian is to accommodate them both. I don't like to brag, but according to my Aunt Rosa, who's the genealogist of the family, we're related to St. Francis of Assisi."

"Wow!"

He looked at me a moment as if he'd just had the

brightest idea since the invention of pizza. But then he shook his head. "I'd offer one of them to you, George—is it okay if I call you George upon such short acquaintance?"

"Please do, Mr. Anthony."

"It's Don to people I like."

I wondered what he had found likable about me, but I was grateful anyhow.

"As I was about to say, George, I don't think, upon further reflection, that introducing you to one of these broads would quite work out, though I'm sure you still have a lot of juice left in the old kazoo." He grinned down at my crotch.

I tried to look modest. Actually, I didn't have anything there to brag about, either as to size or performance. Unlike the characters in the Jacqueline Susann novel, *Once Is Not Enough,* once was usually sufficient for my wife, Alice, and me. Only rarely would we go for an encore. On birthdays and our wedding anniversary. Valentine's Day. And special occasions like that.

"That's okay," I said. "I know I'm probably too old and plain looking for the ladies of your acquaintance. Thanks anyhow for the kind thought."

"Don't mention it. Actually, I don't think you're all that ancient looking. Have you ever thought of using Grecian Formula 16? My Uncle Gino swears by it, and rightly so, because he's been shacking up with a broad as young as his daughter. In fact, the two bimbos were in the same confirmation class in Yonkers. You wouldn't believe this, but afterward, at the gala reception, even though it was around Lent, the nuns served bagels instead of hot-cross buns."

"With cream cheese and lox?"

"Only cream cheese."

I shook my head and sighed. "We're certainly living in a different world."

"You can say that again. No respect for tradition, even if it's a Jewish tradition. Speaking of the past, if you don't mind older broads of about forty or maybe fifty without the makeup, there's one down the corridor here, probably a former debutante, who I could probably fix you up with before you can say 'Ronald Reagan reaped a row of rotten raspberries' three times. Last night when we were in the elevator, she leaned against my cock and...."

I listened politely to the rest of Don's story about the former debutante, but I really wasn't all that enthralled. Though I won't deny that sex is here to stay, the raunchy kind has always made me uncomfortable.

Don looked up from his gold watch. "Well, it was nice doing business with you, George."

"It was a mutual pleasure, I'm sure. About the tab for the weapon...."

Suavely, he drew a hand through the air to convey that I was to think no more about it. "I'll bill Big Nick according to our customary arrangement."

I nodded, and after picking up my hat and coat from a chair, I took a last look at the picture over the bed. It showed a man and woman in silk costumes sitting on a white bench in the shadow of tall trees that reached up to the sky. Valentine's Day was coming up, and I wondered how much such a picture would cost, a reproduction rather than an original. I was sorry I had turned out to be such a disappointment to Alice. At least, as a breadwinner. Even before her Aunt Patty was falsely accused of shoplifting a Sinatra album from Macy's after previous success with Tony Martin and Tony Bennett, Alice had always had a fixation about avoiding trouble with the law. And afraid that it would threaten our relationship, I hadn't told her that I was desperate enough to go to work for Big Nick.

Don preceded me to the door with the same brisk steps of the banker to whom I had years ago applied for a mortgage loan. It was before Alice returned to the business world after raising the kids. The banker turned me down because of insufficient income and assets. Other banks also turned me down, and so we were stuck in an apartment on Avenue U instead of being able to move out to the fresh air on Long Island. The neighborhood got worse and worse, including porno at our local movie house, but we'd never been able to get away from it. I marched in the anti-porno demonstration that was led by Chuck Schumer, a local politician. The porno ended, but the theater closed and never reopened.

"If I may ask," Don said, "have you ever used a .38?"

"Sure, but not in quite a while. It all comes back to you, I hear. Like playing dominos or riding a bike."

"First chance you get, take a few practice shots at your worst enemy. I ain't kidding. Nothing ventured, nothing gained."

From his voice and look, I couldn't tell whether he was being serious. As for me, since I had no idea that I would so soon, within hours, be running into my worst enemy in all the world, I was certainly joking as I said, "Sounds like a terrific idea."

"Go for it."

"Absolutely."

He opened the door and shook my hand as genially as if he'd just sold me a car that was a lemon. "See you again when you're in the market for a semiautomatic or assault rifle. 'Onward and upward' is the motto of the builders of the World Trade Center, or so I once read in *The Wall Street Journal,* where I keep track of my securities. Everything I sell has the seal of approval of Bruce Willis and Clint Eastwood." He winked. "Please convey my deepest regards to Big Nick when you see him."

I said that it would be my great pleasure, and then the door clicked behind me and I started up the corridor to the elevator. Ringing in my ears was what Big Nick had told me many times in recent weeks: "Even on days that we don't go to church, we should get down on our knees and thank God that America is still a land of opportunities unlimited."

First I held my portfolio against my side by a few fingers, but the gun kept banging against my leg, and so

I finally placed it under my arm, the way portfolios are often carried on Madison Avenue and Wall Street, both of which areas I used to visit often as a messenger for an outfit called Empire Courier. It was incredible that thirty-two years had passed since then, and the thought made me want to weep, but then I remembered the wise words of a friend, Ed Burke, who was a leader in Alcoholics Anonymous: "Never cry over spilled milk. Go out and buy yourself a fresh container."

In a way, my forthcoming job with Big Nick was my other container of milk, and as I walked to the elevator, I resolved to think more positively from now on. My Aunt Frances had been a hotel chambermaid for many years until one morning, on the day before Christmas to be exact, she was fired because she couldn't help getting old and arthritic, and so I made a nice smile to a black woman with a bundle of towels over her arm. She was still young and very pretty and well supplied in the bosom, and I wondered why she was making beds for strangers while less-attractive women were married to wealthy men or established in profitable jobs. Was a capacity for success something like blue eyes and dimples, which some people had and others didn't?

"I can do your room now," the chambermaid chirped like so many newcomers from the Caribbean. "May I have your number, please?"

I tapped my portfolio as if I was an architect and it contained the blueprints for my latest skyscraper on Park

Avenue or wherever. "Merely visiting on some business." I tried to speak more elegantly than usual, as if I had taken the speech course once offered evenings at Madison High. Chuck Schumer, the anti-porno guy, may well have taken it, because he was now a state assemblyman and was a favorite to become our next congressman in Washington.

"Have a nice day, sir."

"You too, miss." On an impulse, though I knew it was old fashioned and gauche, I tipped my hat the way the Honorable Thomas X. Mahoney used to greet voters whenever he and his mistress and her Shih Tzu emerged from the Seth Low Regular Democratic Club on Coney Island Avenue. When the mistress was hit by a car outside Molly Murphy's Pub and had to move far away to Florida for her health and maybe her life, I was not the only one who wondered whether a local hood had gotten a contract from the not-so-honorable *Mrs.* Thomas X. Mahoney.

The maid's smile broadened as she turned away, and I hoped that my little courtesy had made her day, just as her mistaking me for a Plaza guest had given me a little lift though I needed much more. On my way along the corridor, enjoying the thick carpet underfoot, I kept hoping that Don's former debutante wouldn't open a door and beckon to me with a curling finger. I had never really felt comfortable with that kind of woman, although, of course, I knew they had their charms with other men. To tell the truth, Alice was the only woman I had ever been to bed with. At least, since we started to date. And even before that I was never exactly Brooklyn's answer to Don Juan or Casanova.

Waiting for the elevator, I began to wonder whatever became of all the elevator operators who used to work in the Globe Building until it was automated, leaving only Ben the starter with a job. During one of our recent chats, Big Nick had said that he looked forward to the day when his own business could be fully automated and computerized, just like mortgage loans will soon be handled at some of the banks. For instance, a client for a rubout would sit down at a computer and type out the name and some data about the desired victim, whether a rival in business or in an affair of the heart, as they say. If the order was approved, the client would be quoted a fee payable at once by a credit card from American Express or Diners Club, and that would be that. No extras for taxes or shipping and handling, as, I am sure, a mail order from Sears or Montgomery Ward would charge.

Over a glass of wine, Big Nick assured me that I had the makings of a good hitman even though I would be starting out a little late in life.

"You look mature and respectable," he said, "and you can get into places where some of my young punks would stick out like a topless nun in St. Patrick's Cathedral. Naturally, I have contacts with practitioners who look more respectable than justices on the Supreme Court, or any of those other greedy scumbags in Washington, but they are very pricey, as you can well imagine. To be candid, I think you would do very well in some of the medium-range jobs, such as knocking off businessmen whose wives have gotten the hots for younger guys who will screw them round the clock like maybe Robert Redford or Tony Curtis in the movies. Or so they hope, the dumb cunts. Due maybe to women's lib, it's become a real growth industry in the last few years." He shook his head and sighed. "Though I consider myself a good Catholic, I wish I could feel a little more compassion and empathy for Wendy Frick, that dumb little whore in Westchester who's been in the news and may spend the rest of her life in the slammer. Instead of spending a few bucks and getting a pro who would do the job right, she tried to take care of her boyfriend's wife on her own. Especially for a laywoman, poison is no longer the way to go, not since Governor Carey increased the budget for forensic labs all over the state."

"I appreciate the vote of confidence, but what I really came to you for was a job as a clerk or something in one of your legit businesses. Or with a friend."

After showing me the fancy label on the bottle, he poured us another drink of wine. Then he put an arm around my shoulders and looked at me as if I were wacky or on a new and improved kind of marijuana called maybe Dreaming of Marilyn.

"Those are shit jobs. All your life you worked at that shit job at the *Globe* and look what you have to show for it. At fifty, they throw you out on your ass and replace you with a broad."

"That wasn't it exactly. I wasn't fired. I left of my own volition."

"I think you're being technical. From what you've told me, this scumbag Warren made it so unpleasant for you that you had to save your self-respect and call it a day there."

"That's true," I admitted.

"If I'd been aware of your situation, I would have sent an education committee around to the *Globe*. And they would have started, as usual, with a basic course that would be called Cemeteries 101 in a catalogue from NYU, my daughter's school. Anyhow, the bottom line is that I won't have an old buddy of mine working in a shit job without a future. According to my statistics, you have at least ten productive years ahead of you. Ralph Tornadello was doing some of his best work for me when he was sixty, and he would probably be working still if things hadn't gone a little haywire on his last job." He smiled, then looked upward as if in his mind's eye he could clearly see Ralph Tornadello with wings and a harp. "But he had a first-class funeral with a beautiful Mass that went straight up to St. Peter like, in the old days, a homer by Joe DiMaggio into the left-field stands. I asked Father Angelo to go all out for him, as I do for all my guys. Unfortunately, my favorite baritone, Mario Pucelli, had a long-standing commitment to do *Tosca* in Rio, but we did have the tenor who'll be as good as Pavarotti in a few years if he doesn't die first from an overdose of pasta."

Finally the elevator arrived, carrying only a fat man in a homburg and a black overcoat such as Mr. Drew, the publisher of the *Globe*, used to wear upon occasion. As I joined him in the car, he shifted to the side as if I might contaminate him with my six-year-old topcoat that wasn't from Brooks Brothers but a place called Irving's on Kings Highway. Alice called it "tacky" and kept urging me to buy a new one, but at the sales I visited from time to time, I never liked the ones in my price range.

My fellow passenger was carrying a leather attaché case as shiny as his shoes, and he glanced contemptuously at my portfolio. I wondered what he would think if he knew what was inside it, though, for all I knew, he was one of Big Nick's expensive hit men on his way to a job.

When in Big Nick's employ, there would no doubt be occasions when I would have to kill a guy in an elevator. I now imagined what it would be like if I were on a job right here, and the look of surprise on his smug face as I unzipped my portfolio and whipped out my gun.

"No! Don't!" he would scream. "You have the wrong man. I'll give you all my money. I'll order my beautiful blond daughter to go to bed with you. I have a mother, wife and children to support. Though I'm dressed up, I'm a fellow Democrat. Are you a Catholic? So am I. Hail Mary, full of grace. Are you Jewish? *Shalom aleichem.* I contributed a thousand dollars to Israel during the war against the Arabs."

In my intense excitement I began to perspire, and I

would have mopped my brow if I had had a neat handkerchief instead of crushed tissues in my pocket. My fellow passenger was staring at me, and so I said, "It's hot here, isn't it?"

"If you'd just come back from Alaska, as I have, I'm sure you would appreciate the heat."

I doubted that he had ever been closer to Alaska than the deep freezer in his basement. Obviously, he was just one of those people who had to have the last word on every subject.

When the elevator stopped and the door opened, he rushed past me as if he had a legal or natural right to exit first. I felt like kicking him in the behind, for which I was in a perfect position. While I was still in the car, people began to pile in, and I had to push my way out like on a subway train at the height of the rush hour.

"You can say 'excuse me,'" said a white-haired woman who resembled an older version of Sandra Blaine, the *Globe*'s society writer and expert on gracious living, although she used foul language and her desk and office were always a mess.

I wasn't aware that I had stepped on her toes or anything, but I turned round and said, "Excuse me, please, madam."

She whirled away as if I had made an indecent proposition to her.

"Screw you, sister," I said under my breath. I knew that she wouldn't have been so rude to me if I were a man who traveled in her own social circles and gave off that glow of success and wealth. Big Nick was right, as usual. He had once told me that only with guns and threats could ordinary people like us, descended from immigrants, make an impression on the high and mighty.

Interested in my progress, he had instructed me to give him a call when I got my gun, and this I now proceeded to do in the lobby. When I had trouble locating an outside phone and finally had to ask for help from the usual greedy-looking bellhop, I hoped that he wasn't expecting a tip for this common courtesy. I wanted to tell him I wasn't a millionaire rancher from Texas but only a fellow workingman, and unemployed, and not even getting unemployment insurance, thanks to incredible meanness by my former employer. Since Big Nick's phone was almost certainly being bugged, I was to use a phony name and certain code expressions. It didn't faze me at all. From bitter experience I knew that every business has its own lies and shenanigans. In my first job, at a fruit and vegetable store, I had had to check that each box of strawberries contained its quota of rotten ones on the bottom. And I had to warn women who inspected inside the boxes that they were spreading deadly germs and that my boss had a legal responsibility to report them to the Board of Health. In my most recent job, at the *Globe,* I once learned that Mel Pierce sent his own kids to an exclusive all-white private school in New Rochelle while in his popular, bleeding-heart editorials he used to cry out that integrated public schools were the only salvation of the city and the nation.

"Good morning," I said to Big Nick. "This is Tim Driscoll." I would never know why he had chosen this Irish name for me.

"And a good morning to you, Mr. Driscoll. It's nice to hear your fine Irish voice again. How's your cat coming along?"

"I took him this morning to that vet you suggested. The vet says he'll be fine."

"Good. He's a swell doctor and did wonders for my wife's Siamese. Just don't feed the animal too much today. I think eight sardines should be sufficient, and let me suggest, if I may, Salvatore's Portuguese sardines in olive oil."

Which meant that I was to meet him at eight at Sal's Grotto on Bleecker Street in Greenwich Village. Then, either there or at one of Big Nick's other joints in the area, he would formally swear me into his family, from which there could never be resignation or desertion. Usually, there had to be an investigation period of a few weeks, like when you're applying for a passport or charge account at Saks Fifth Avenue, but Big Nick had assured his council of elders that my credentials were of the highest order.

"I think eight's about the right number," I said. "Please give my regards to your charming wife."

"And mine to yours. It was a pleasure speaking to you again."

"Likewise, I'm sure."

I saw my hand shaking as I put down the phone. What the hell was I doing here at the Plaza? What was I getting myself into? The money would be good, but money wasn't everything in this world, though it was certainly a lot, especially when you weren't well educated or handsome or witty or charming and you were fifty years old.

How I wished that I still had someone wise and sympathetic like Father Daniel to counsel me. In the distant past when he was still alive and doing the Lord's work at St. Peter's on Avenue Y, he used to dwell mostly on his favorite vices, masturbation and intoxication, but I was sure he would have had some insights into my present dilemma. Of course, he would have told me to stay far away from Big Nick. It's always so easy to give good advice to the other guy, but the church itself always accepted Big Nick's contributions to schools and charities, and such personal favors as tickets to ball games and vouchers for the hotels and casinos in Atlantic City.

As usual, my emotional distress gave me an urge to visit the bathroom, and I thought that I might as well do it in style here at the Plaza. Though I was by no means an habitué of the hotel, I knew from my sightseeing strolls with Alice where the bathroom was. As I entered, the attendant was standing by the basins and reading the *Daily News*. He turned to smile me his best wishes for a smooth sailing, but I avoided eye contact with him, because I didn't intend to afterward accept one of his monogrammed hand towels and tip him at least a quarter, which I assumed was the minimum.

I was afraid I would drop the portfolio and damage the gun as I unbuttoned my coat and unzipped. The attendant rushed forward to relieve me of the portfolio, but I turned my head and gestured that I was self-sufficient and okay. Damn it, I had established eye contact, after all.

I had told Big Nick that a conversation about a sick cat would be too corny for words, but he had replied that talking about helpless animals might improve his image with the cops or the Feds in case they were wasting taxpayers' money by bugging him again. While I did my thing in the urinal, I remembered after forty-five years the time that Molly, our white cat, gave birth to a litter and my father called the ASPCA to take them all away. I didn't know of my father's treachery until the man from the ASPCA arrived with a large wooden box that resembled the picture of President Lincoln's log cabin in my coloring book. He waited at the door for my father to bring out the four kittens from their carton near the stove in the kitchen. I cried and begged and screamed and kicked on the floor that I didn't want the kittens to be taken away and killed. My father said that we couldn't keep more than one cat in the small apartment, and when I wouldn't stop crying, he slapped me around a little and locked me up in the bedroom. Through the door he shouted that if I didn't behave, he would give me away to the gypsies who had recently moved into a store down the block. I didn't really believe he would do it, but you never can tell about parents. Or, for that matter, about anyone else.

Afterward, I wouldn't talk to my father for many days, and I didn't really forgive him for a couple of years, not until his doctor at Coney Island Hospital allowed me to come into his ward and visit him on his deathbed. His face and hands were as white as his pillowcase and sheets. He tried to smile, and I tried to smile back, hoping he understood that I forgave him everything. He withdrew a hand from under the sheet and motioned me with a finger to bring my head closer, and, after taking a deep breath, he patted my head for the first time ever and whispered that I was to be a good boy, go to church every Sunday, and make my mother proud of me. About an hour later, I was reading a Superman comic book I had found in the waiting room downstairs when I saw Mama come out of the elevator crying and screaming, and I knew it was all over and that he was now, as I had once been taught by Sister Angelica, a bambino again and in heaven with his Mama and Papa and Jesus and Mary and all the saints.

My business at the urinal was over too, and as I turned and saw the attendant holding out his towel, I didn't have the heart to just walk past him as if he were a nonperson in the eyes of the world, just like I myself had become. After washing my hands, I dried them more thoroughly than usual, wanting to get my money's worth out of the towel. The attendant started to brush my coat with great devotion as if I were off to see Queen Elizabeth like in a documentary on Channel Thirteen, but, afraid he would expect a second quarter, I shook my head that it was unnecessary.

"No important business conferences this morning," I said, and dropped a quarter and, what the hell, an additional two nickels into a bowl with the hotel's crest.

"No, sir," he said, his dentures clicking. His smile added that not even his regular visitors had important business conferences every morning for which they had to be spruced up to the nines. He was a scrawny, bent-over man of about seventy, bald except for gray wisps hanging over his large, protruding ears. I wondered about the chain of events that had led to this humiliating job in a men's room, even though it was at the Plaza and not a whorehouse in Hell's Kitchen. Surely, in his youth in Italy or wherever, he had had the usual high hopes of conquering the world, whether by fair means or foul. As if he were reading my embarrassing thoughts about him, he turned away from me suddenly. Then he pushed up his eyeglasses and began to polish the mirror over a basin.

"Have a nice day," he said.

"Thank you. You too. *Buon giorno*," I added, because it seemed the friendly and Italian thing to do.

Outside in the corridor I passed a shop window with old Longines and Omega watches that were being recycled as "treasures from the past." It made me sad to think that older people never increased in value like these watches, or like real estate or works of art. I had two good kids, as kids went nowadays, and they phoned regularly, James from Florida and Rosemary from Ohio, but they had outgrown me even before leaving home, using words I didn't understand, referring to people, places and things I had never heard of, sometimes making fun of things I considered thoughtful and polite, such as my once sending a Hallmark greeting card to Joan Fontaine, one of my favorite movie stars since seeing her in *The Constant Nymph* and *Jane Eyre* when I was a kid. I had read that she was suffering severe depression because she had been rejected for a minor though respectable role in a remake of a film in which she had once starred, and depression was a condition I knew a lot about.

The main lobby was so warm and pleasant, radiating a mood that life was beautiful, that I hated to leave it. Many years ago, after a visit to Central Park, Alice and I had passed through at a time of day when the Palm Court was open for business and the musicians were playing "The Merry Widow Waltz," which I had first heard in Miss Plish's music appreciation class at Cunningham Junior High. She had also introduced us to, among other compositions, *The 1812 Overture* by Tchaikovsky, and Beethoven's *Pastoral Symphony,* and Ravel's *Bolero.*

"There's a menu on that stand," I had said to Alice. "Let's go over and see the prices, not for a main dish but for cake and coffee, if they do serve just cake and coffee."

"It's crazy," Alice said, but her big brown eyes were

sparkling like the sunshine on the lake back at Maxwell's Lodge in the Poconos, our honeymoon retreat where we couldn't retreat from "I Want to Hold Your Hand," a Beatles song that was played day and night on the PA. If I remember correctly, the desserts at the Palm Court were in the seven-dollar range, and plain coffee and tea were in the five. We retreated to a spot where the haughty maître d' couldn't overhear our financial discussion, not that he could possibly be interested in us.

"It's crazy," Alice said again.

"You only live once," I said, and added wittily, "unless you're from India and believe in reincarnation. With my luck, I'd come back as a bedbug."

"Look at the bright side, honey. You might be a bedbug here at the Plaza. Or at the White House."

"I would prefer the Plaza. You never know who the president is going to be."

We took our place in line behind the plush rope with all the other *bon vivants,* and later on a stunning redhead in black satin emerged from the Palm Court and asked us with her nose in the air, "How many?"

"Two, please."

She shook her head. "Sorry. I have a table for four."

The group directly behind us was a foursome—a man and woman and two boys with fresh haircuts and wearing dark blazers with elaborate gold crests, just like the boys in *Goodbye, Mr. Chips.* They left the line and followed the hostess into the Palm Court.

"If the kids were with us," Alice said, "we could be going in now."

"If the kids were with us," I reminded her, "we all four couldn't afford to eat here."

"I'm not sure even the two of us can afford it," she said. "Tuesday is rent day, and Friday is the day I visit the dentist and maybe learn that I need a crown. Or even root canal, which I always thought was only for the rich and famous."

Across the rope, we saw a man slip a folded bill to the maître d', who looked as suave as Bela Lugosi in *Dracula* when he wasn't sucking a woman's blood and turning her into a vampire. And a minute later we saw a departing guest casually peel a few bills from his wad and toss them on a table. A man handed a bill to the violinist, who snatched it with two fingers and didn't miss a note of "The Emperor Waltz" by Strauss, which I also first heard in junior high. I wondered if the violinist could have handled a charge card from the Diners Club.

The redhead returned, smiling, overjoyed at our good luck. "I have a nice table for two now."

Suddenly I got cold feet about this whole enterprise, and I looked at my Timex and said, "My Lord! I really don't think we have the time now."

"No," Alice agreed. "We have that engagement with the Carlsons for six, and it's all the way up in Westchester."

"Pleasantville," I confirmed.

As we joined hands and left the line, I glanced over

my shoulder to see who would be going into the Palm Court in our place, and it was a tall couple with a guy who looked like Cary Grant, and both had suntans as if they had spent a lot of time at a luxurious resort. On the subway home, we promised ourselves we would return to the Palm Court upon a later occasion when I had advanced at the *Globe* and money was no problem. Back in Brooklyn, at Sherman's bakery on Avenue U, we bought a raisin cake that looked vaguely like a miniature version of one of the cakes that had been displayed under a dome cover at the Palm Court. But, somehow, we never returned there.

This morning, the tables were being set with linen and silverware by Orientals in white jackets and black bowties, and, across the floor at the piano, a musician was striking a single key while he decided if it needed a tuning. With the hand movements of a band leader, a brunette in a black jumpsuit supervised the transfer of cakes from a pair of delivery carts to the display table. She was appalled by the result, and commented to her subordinates, "Somehow, it doesn't make me drool. Especially with the new prices going into effect today."

One of the subordinates told her, "No sweat. Just wait till we've arranged the kiwi tarts. They'll make a world of difference. I give you my word. Anyhow, what would tourists know about old prices and new prices?"

"You're right, Manuel. With that sunny disposition of yours, you should have been a shrink."

"Your shrink, I hope."

She giggled. "Shame on you."

And so I bid a fond farewell to the Plaza, as they used to say about Samoa in the Fitzpatrick travelogues at the Loew's Kings a long, long time ago. At the revolving door I stepped aside for a dowager. I assumed she was a dowager because she wore a mink coat, and looked very old despite her ton of makeup, and she carried a white poodle probably named Fifi or Yvonne.

"Nice doggy," I said, and tried to pat its head.

Animals usually return my affection, but this one tried to bite my hand.

"Emily doesn't like to be petted by strangers," the dowager informed me with a smile.

"I can certainly see that." On the steps outside, I remembered a Quotable Quote from a *Reader's Digest* I once read in a chiropractor's waiting room, and I observed to the dowager, "'Strangers are friends we haven't met yet.'"

"That's very profound, sir. Are you a clergyman, may I ask?"

"No, I happen to be a layman," I said, and tipped my hat as she turned away.

Since she seemed to be a kindly old soul, I thought of following her down the steps and telling her I was unemployed, and asking whether her husband had a job for me in one of his far-flung enterprises. I appreciated Big Nick's offer, but couldn't help feeling that I should be in another line of endeavor. With my lousy luck, I would suffer the fate of Ralph Tornadello on my very first assignment.

But the dowager was already crossing the sidewalk toward the open door of her limousine, a black Mercedes almost as long as a hearse, and it somehow had a chilling effect on me. I decided to invest in a copy of the *Times* and make one last stab at finding something legit, even if it was a shit job. I buttoned up my coat and started for the newsstand down on Fifty-ninth and Madison.

Across the street from the Plaza, something was going on near the fountain that always reminded Alice and me of a wedding cake though not of our own. It turned out to be the shooting of a TV commercial for a Buick Electra. Surrounded by a cameraman and an army of technicians and staff, enough people for a sequel to *Gone with the Wind*, a young man who looked like Congressman Dan Quayle was opening the door of the Buick for a blonde in a fur coat. She kissed his cheek, gazed adoringly at the car as if it made her life complete, and then she slithered inside, meanwhile raising her coat for an exposure of her shapely legs. The implication of her action seemed to be that she would soon expose much more of herself to the thoughtful owner of this elegant car.

"Cut!" yelled a man in a sheepskin coat and jeans, and he went into a huddle with the two actors. When he pointed to the woman's legs, she shrugged, giggled and shook her fanny like Marilyn Monroe in *Some Like It Hot*.

I had read somewhere that the current trend in commercials was to hire non-actors, plain men and women in the street, and so I tried to get closer to the action, hoping that a producer or someone would notice me and consider me ideal for a detergent commercial, or one where I could stand at a counter and look confused about the various brands of toothpaste until the genial pharmacist put me wise to Crest or Colgate's. My heart beat faster as a young man in a red down coat started toward me. I turned my head so that he could see my profile, upon which I had received a compliment or two in my day, long ago but not all that far away in Brooklyn.

"We're shooting in this area. Would you mind moving on?"

With a wave of his clipboard he indicated the direction in which he desired me to go, which would ultimately land me into the line of traffic on Fifth Avenue. I nodded, started away, and then worked up the courage to return and say: "Can you use an extra?"

"An extra what?"

"An extra actor. What else?"

"Not at the present moment, thank you."

"Do you expect to need one in the near future on other commercials?"

"I believe we're well supplied with talent for the foreseeable future. Thanks for your interest, though. And now...." He waved his clipboard again, faster, and closer to my face.

"That's a nice car you've got," I said, stalling for time, hoping that one of the other TV people would see me and recognize my potential.

"I'll convey your sentiments to the good people at Buick and GM."

As I stood my ground, he looked off toward a husky guy in a black leather jacket who might well have been a moonlighting cop. He looked as menacing as Charles Bronson in *Death Wish,* and being in possession of an illegal firearm, I was not in a strong position to defend my prerogative as a citizen to occupy a public thoroughfare, and so I said goodbye and hurried away. I'm sure he thought I was a starry-eyed jerk, but nothing ventured, nothing gained.

Waiting for the light to change on Fifth Avenue, I saw a Rolls-Royce go by, and I strongly doubted that Alice and I would ever get to London and see Buckingham Palace and the Houses of Parliament. I was glad we had gotten to Disney World while we had the chance. I had felt a real sense of accomplishment when, after the trip, James came home from school and said that he was the only kid in his class who had ever been there except for Bernice Demco, the daughter of a local undertaker who once got a terrific write-up in the *Brooklyn Chronicle* after, by no coincidence, he signed up for ads in their weekend magazine section.

I spotted a lucky penny as I crossed the avenue. The penny turned out to be unlucky for me. Bending down for it, I suffered a spasm in the right shoulder where I had recently had a touch of bursitis. The pain became so excruciating that I thought I should enter the General

Motors showroom across the street and sit down on one of the benches I remembered there from visits with the kids, always a highlight of our thrifty excursions to Manhattan.

There were plenty of seats in the vast hall, but no vacant benches where I could sit down alone with my misery, and I plopped down at the end of one that was occupied by a woman of about forty-five, very plainly dressed in a white knit hat and a maroon coat. Only after I had already sat down and saw her glance at me did it occur to me to say, "I hope this seat isn't taken, madam." I placed my hand with the wedding band on my lap to indicate delicately that I was a married man and had no sexual designs on her. Truthfully, she was not very attractive with her sharp nose and resemblance to Miss Wallace, a scolding teacher I had once had. And even if I were not happily married, I would not have wished to make her acquaintance.

"Oh, no, it isn't," she replied, and she smiled to convey that she appreciated my courtesy.

Having concluded this formality, I closed my eyes and prayed for my pain to subside. Usually, I carried around a pill bottle with assorted tablets for my various afflictions—spastic colon, muscular spasms, rheumatoid arthritis, intercostal neuralgia, you name it—but this morning I had forgotten to transfer it from my everyday parka to my special-occasion topcoat. Even without a pill, the pain lessened in a few minutes, but it didn't go away entirely, and I thought I would sit there awhile and enjoy the warmth and the quiet. As the former owner of a used Chevy that had given me only twelve miles to a gallon, I hardly felt that I was abusing the hospitality of General Motors.

With my eyes closed, I hadn't been aware that the woman was watching me, but she evidently was, because I heard her saying: "Excuse me for asking, but are you in pain?"

"Not really," I said, opening my eyes. But seeing her sympathetic expression, I added, "Well, yes, I am, but it's nothing to write home about."

Her brow creasing, she raised a hand to her lips as if I had mentioned a fatal disease. "I'm sorry," she whispered with a sad smile.

"It's nothing, really, and I appreciate your kind concern. I get this shoulder trouble every once in a while, and eventually it goes away. The pain, not the shoulder." I made a little laugh.

She touched her shoulder as if she were a fellow sufferer, and then looked off toward a black Cadillac being polished by an attendant. It looked fine to me, but he kept on polishing and polishing, as if the head of GM might drop in with a gadget that measured brightness.

"What do you think of the styles this season?" she asked.

"They look more sumptuous than ever, I would say. Of course, the prices could be a little more reasonable, but I don't think that'll happen in my lifetime."

"You never can tell."

"That's true, of course. You never can tell about anything."

"Have you made your selection yet?"

"Not really. I'm just browsing today, you might say."

"So am I," she informed me.

She folded her hands upon her lap and stared thoughtfully for a while at the conscientious attendant, who seemed likely to rub off the paint if he continued much longer. Finally she turned her head to me again and said, "By the way, I am Mrs. Forester."

"How do you do. I am Mr. Mancuso."

"How do you do. I rather thought you might be Italian. Something about your eyes. I have many pleasant memories of Italy, which I visited three times with my late husband."

"I haven't been there once yet, but my wife and I are meaning to go one of these years."

"Don't put it off too long. It's a trip everyone should take at least once in a lifetime."

"So I've been told."

"No doubt you've been postponing your trip for reasons of business."

"Something like that."

Mrs. Forester nodded that she understood. "Business is important, but so is culture, and broadening one's understanding of the world."

"That's true."

"This spring and summer, I would suggest, if I may, that you forget the office for once and sail forth to the horizon."

"I think maybe I will. Thank you for the advice."

Blinking, she removed a tissue from her coat pocket and pressed it to the corner of her eye. Next she pressed a hand to her throat while she slowly turned her head away. "I have few consolations in my life," she said softly, "but one of them is that John and I visited Italy and Egypt and all those other wonderful places when we did. Our last residence was in Schenectady, though we were both born and bred here in New York. Washington Heights, to be exact. Named for George Washington, the father of our country. Yesterday I returned to New York to attend to a few matters pursuant to settling John's estate, what was left of it. This morning, having some time left before my departure, I did a little shopping—mostly window shopping—on the East Side. The *Upper* East Side, of course."

"Of course," I murmured, conscious that Alice and I occasionally shopped on Orchard Street, which was on the *Lower* East Side and famous for bargains. In fact, I was wearing today just a slightly imperfect Rogers Peet tie that, instead of a dollar, would have cost at least fifteen dollars at their fancy store on Fifth Avenue.

Mrs. Forester's purse had been lying across her thighs, and now she pressed the clasp and opened it. "At Bloomingdale's, when I reached in for my wallet to pay for a purchase, I became aware that it was gone."

"Maybe you left it at your hotel room."

"No, I had it earlier at the gift shop of the Metropolitan Museum of Art," she said, and lifted a plastic shopping bag from the other side of her. "But the money is really the least of my loss."

"Charge cards?"

"Both Bloomingdale's and Lord & Taylor. Plus all sorts of identification. Plus a few irreplaceable pictures of John and some dear friends." She heaved a sigh. "Thank God I paid for my hotel room the first thing this morning."

"Thank God. Did you report your loss?"

"Both to the stores and to the police, but a Sergeant Delaney was not very hopeful."

"You never can tell." I tried but failed to think of an inspiring quote from *Reader's Digest*.

"That's so very true. But meanwhile," she said, putting her hands to her temples, "I have no friends or family in town, and I don't even have the modest fare of $25.80 to get back to Schenectady, where I reside presently."

I wanted to slap my head and groan. Or scream at the top of my lungs. With all the empty seats in the showroom, I had sat down on the same bench with Gertie the Con. At least, that's what Stan Schultz, one of the *Globe*'s local reporters, had called her in his feature story about three years ago. Everything matched with Stan's description of the woman and her modus operandi. The eminently respectable and ladylike appearance. The late husband. And the need of bus or train fare back home to a distant city, but not so distant as to dry up a victim's stream of generosity.

She slid toward me on the bench and touched my hand. Her hand was smoother than Alice's, probably because with her ill-gotten gains she could afford a servant to do her cleaning and washing. She turned an anguished face at me, and, her voice thick and choked, she said: "Though it's true that our acquaintance is on the brief side, far briefer than in that wonderful English movie by Noel Coward, I feel that we have developed a deep empathy, and I have the confidence to ask you to extend me the little loan I need in order to return home. Naturally, I shall mail you a check, special delivery, as soon as I reach Schenectady this afternoon."

I looked at my watch and pretended to be shocked by the time. "Wow!" I said, and jumped to my feet. "I didn't realize it was so late. I have an urgent business appointment way out on Long Island."

Gertie did not look so very surprised by my action. She gave a pained smile and, still sitting, reached for my hand. I thrust it into my pocket.

"Oh, dear me," she said. "I was so afraid that you might misconstrue, and I can't say that I blame you, Mr. Mancuso. Naturally, you are uncertain of my sincerity and veracity. But for the paltry sum involved, won't you take a chance on human nature and give me the benefit of the doubt? Our Lord Jesus said: 'As you give, so shall it be given unto you.' Don't you believe that's true? Please don't disappoint me, for the sake of your immortal soul. Pope John Paul would send you his blessing if he knew of your fine Christian deed."

All my life I have been awkward at breaking off conversations, both on the phone and in person. Feeling a few coins in my coat pocket, I pulled them out and thrust them at her. She jerked back as if I were a flasher and had shown her my penis.

"Oh, no!" she cried, a hand to her bosom, guarding her virtue or self-respect. "I don't want charity. I asked only for a loan for the sake of our Lord."

"I'm sorry. This is all I can afford today. Have a nice day," I said, and started to back away from her.

"I'm really very disappointed in you, Mr. Mancuso."

As she suddenly turned her head sharply and purposefully to the left, I turned in that direction too, and saw a tall man in a tan trench coat standing in a corner near an ugly plant with the long stiff shoots that are popular in funeral parlors, maybe because they do not wilt or die like humans. As he began to approach us with the air of an authority figure, I instinctively disliked him. I didn't like his long sideburns like a tango dancer's, and I disliked the curl of hair covering half of his brow. I knew he represented trouble for me. My portfolio was under my arm. Slowly I lowered it and put my hand on the zipper tab.

"Something going on here?" he asked in a slick voice. "I'm Special Officer Tracy. Let's keep our voices down.

After all, this showroom has been described as a cathedral of commerce."

"I'm so glad you're here, Officer Tracy," Gertie said in a genteel squeak. "The Good Lord has sent you to me."

"I can see you're upset, madam, but try to keep your self-control and composure."

Before speaking, she clenched her hands together and placed them over her crotch. "This man, whom I don't know at all, has just made an indecent proposal to me. I'm a respectable married woman. My husband has a responsible job with Merrill Lynch on Wall Street. I'm sure you've heard of them. Mary Martin deals with them. Or so I recall from an ad I once saw. My husband and I just adored her in *The Sound of Music*."

Officer Tracy nodded that this was certainly important evidence, and then he turned to me and shook his head in reproach. "This is a most serious charge, a violation of article 22.3 of the New York State Criminal Code."

"She's lying," I said.

"I'm shocked," Gertie said. "I belong to the women's auxiliary of my church. The Reverend Woodman will attest to my good character."

"I'm sure we'll straighten this out," Officer Tracy said. He turned back to me and continued, "I'm afraid you'll have to come down to headquarters."

"I'd like to see your ID and badge," I said.

"Take my word for it that my credentials are in perfect order."

"Show 'em to me, anyhow."

Narrowing his eyes, Tracy quickly glanced to his left and right as if he were afraid of our being overheard. This shifty movement told me right away that he was in some shakedown racket with the woman.

"Look here, you disgusting rapist," he snarled under his breath. "I don't want to employ force, but I will if I have to. General Motors is introducing some great, new models and we don't want any bad publicity at this point in time. We all make our little mistakes. Let's go out and discuss this somewhere. You've hurt this good woman's self-respect, and that's a terrible thing. I don't want to throw the book at you, but I do think you should make some restitution to her so that she can hold her head high at the next meeting of the church auxiliary."

Gertie nodded her head, and she said wistfully, "Nothing can really do that after this gross insult, but it might be a lesson to him for the future."

Ordinarily, I would have been nervous and flustered by what was happening to me, but the knowledge that I had a gun in my portfolio gave me courage, and I was more amused than anything else.

"Now let's march out of here real nice and quiet," Tracy advised. "Don't worry, madam," he told Gertie. "I'm sure we'll come to a meeting of the minds."

"Bless you. My next car will certainly be from General Motors. Probably a Chevrolet."

"Right on. General Motors always comes through for

the American public. Just stay away from anything made in Japan or Germany."

"I certainly will. And I still miss those TV commercials with Dinah Shore. It's a great tragedy that she never married Burt Reynolds."

Tracy stepped closer to me. "Okay, fella, let's go before I change my mind and turn you in without further ado."

"No," I said, unzipping my portfolio. "Do you know what I've got inside? A gun. I'm going out of here alone. If either of you con artists tries to stop me or says another word, I'm going to take it out and shoot the living shit out of both of you."

They both turned as white as the tiles back in the bathroom at the Plaza. Tracy stepped back and began to mumble and glare at me. Gertie clasped her hands on her lap and tried to look like a saint who is suffering on behalf of all the sinners of the world.

"What kind of a town has New York become?" she cried. "I warned all my friends that electing Ed Koch as mayor would be a great catastrophe. And I was certainly right."

I backed away a few steps, and then turned and walked to the door, looking over my shoulder to make sure they were both still at the bench. I continued through the door, and once outside, I hurried across GM Plaza and down Fifty-ninth Street, meanwhile zipping up my portfolio. For the first time in many months I had done something truly positive, and I felt proud of myself. I knew it was mostly due to the fact that I had had the gun. And I was sure that I wouldn't have hesitated to use it. All my life people had been taking advantage of me. Maybe what I had always needed was a gun. Maybe Big Nick was right about me. In the Western movies that were usually my favorite part of the Saturday-morning kiddy show at the Avenue U Theater, guns used to be called equalizers. Guys like me needed something to make them feel equal, because we didn't have a fancy education or social connections.

Toward the end of the block I went into a store for a copy of the *Times*. Also on display there was the *Globe*, and I wondered what my career there would have been like if I'd had the courage to stick up for my rights more, if I'd acted with the force and decision I'd just displayed at General Motors. I would never know. Though I'd been on the nicotine wagon since my friend Al Madeiro came down with lung cancer, I also bought a pack of Kents, the brand smoked by my doctor while he wrote out a new prescription for me. Dr. Vogel not only had a mustache like Ronald Colman's but he also held his cigarette in the same sophisticated way.

Suddenly I was feeling devil-may-carish. My life wasn't so valuable to me that I wished to live into old age and become an attendant in a men's room. Aside from the kids and Alice, no one would miss me when I was gone, and even Alice would be better off without me. It had been a mistake for her to marry me, and she was still not too old to find someone else. She still had her looks and charm and smile, and when she dressed up for a gathering, men still ogled her bosom and derriere. I, on the other hand, had declined rapidly in the last few years.

Recently, at the Kingsway Theatre on Coney Island Avenue, the cashier had asked if I was a senior citizen.

"No, I'm not. Do I look like one?"

"I was merely trying to save you two dollars, sir."

"How old do you think I am?"

"I've no idea, really. I'm terrible at ages. Enjoy the show. Next, please."

The man behind me tapped my shoulder and said, "You should have said yes. Better the money in your pocket than in the theater owner's, who will probably send a bigger check to the Republican Party so they can win the next election and end Social Security and Medicare."

On our way to the ticket taker, Alice assured me that to young girls like the cashier everyone with a little gray or a wrinkle looked like a senior citizen.

I tore open my Kents and lit one. After my abstinence of thirty-nine days, the first puffs went to my head at once and I felt dizzy. As I leaned against a shelf of paperbacks, I noticed one that was titled *The Success Imperative* by a Conrad Stevenson, M.D. I pulled it out and read the blurb on the back cover:

Dr. Conrad Stevenson, world-famous psychologist and management consultant, who has helped thousands at his clinic in Baltimore, offers you a proven, step-by-step method for conquering the obstacles in your path to success and happiness.

By learning and applying this common-sense approach to living, you will discover the secrets of creativity, achieve peace of mind and sexual fulfillment, and become a self-respecting, self-reliant human being. Far and away, *The Success Imperative* is the best self-help book that has ever been offered to the public.

I opened the book at random and read: "We must develop our 'success mechanism' just as the runner who aspires to winning the Boston or the New York marathon develops his lungs and thighs. Just as the longest journey begins with a single step, so does success begin with self-acceptance of our present imperfections. Only in this way can we go on to plan reasonable and harmonious goals for ourselves. The secret is to turn around our handicaps and anxieties so that they become directed at goal achievement and not self-destruction. A good plan is to begin with a negative habit such as cigarette smoking. As you light your next cigarette, say to yourself...."

I pulled the disgusting cigarette from my mouth and wondered where Dr. Conrad Stevenson had been all my life. Truly, it was a tragedy that I hadn't discovered his book sooner. How different my life would be today.

I read on page 105: "When oppressed by failures past and present, I meditate on these words by General George C. Marshall: 'When a thing is done, it's done. Don't look back. Look forward to your next objective.'"

That was so very true. I decided to buy the book, and to buy also another book on the same shelf, *Talk Your Way to the Top in Only Twenty-Nine Days* by Suzy Christopher, the prize-winning TV personality and interviewer. The blurb said: "Famous TV talk star Suzy Christopher reveals her personal rules for conversation success as she vividly describes her experiences on-camera and off."

After consulting the table of contents, I opened the book to page 199, the beginning of chapter twelve, "How to Overcome Disaster," which happened to be *my* situation:

"Disaster is when, as happened to famed Finnish distance runner Hilda Schoone, you win the Riviera marathon in the shoes custom-made by your grandfather and then discover that the prize and medal will be awarded by the head of the Nike multinational corporation, which will expect you to praise its footwear products and no one else's."

Well, that wasn't my own disaster exactly, but I was sure that Suzy Christopher had more helpful information for me, and for only a few dollars I couldn't go wrong.

After waiting out three other customers it was finally my turn at the counter, and I put down my two paperbacks and a ten-dollar bill. Suddenly a tall man in

a leather coat and holding a copy of a magazine, *Arts &*
Antiques, appeared from nowhere, thrust a bill at the clerk,
and said to me in a British accent, "Terrible hurry, old
boy. Hope you don't mind. Thank you."

I wondered what Dr. Stevenson and Suzy Christopher would have advised under the circumstances, and
then I said, "No doubt you are, sir, but I happen to be in
a hurry as well. Of course, if it's a life-or-death situation,
then by all means...."

"It is just that," he said. "It very definitely is. You are
so very kind."

The clerk gave him his change and he rushed away.
Awaiting my own change, I responded to the tap on my
shoulder and turned and saw a woman in a black hat with
a long feather.

"If you don't mind my saying so, you shouldn't have
let that Brit get away with that. These foreigners think
they own the city."

"I understand what you mean," I said, using an expression Suzy Christopher would have approved of, "but
I was only being polite."

"You can't be polite with them. They only take advantage of us. For years and years my daughter had an
eye on a certain apartment on West End Avenue. And she
finally thought she was all set to move in. But she didn't
get it. 'Why?' you will ask me."

"Why?" I asked.

"Because a Brazilian from the U.N. bribed the super

and the head of the co-op board. The s.o.b., whose country has been destroying their rain forests and causing air pollution all over the planet, has been in the city for less than a month!"

Nodding that there was profound truth to all she had said, I picked up my bag and said goodbye to her, adding that I hoped her daughter would find a nice apartment soon.

"Not as long as we have all these foreign bloodsuckers!" she cried.

All in all, I thought, my first attempt to apply the principles of Dr. Stevenson and Suzy Christopher hadn't gone too badly. The important thing was to keep practicing. There would have been no sense in being too aggressive with the Englishman. A man merely wants his rights and self-respect, not to become a ball-breaker. I was sure that when he returned to his art gallery or antique shop, the Englishman would remark to his partner or secretary, "Met a rather decent chap in that shop, don't you know. He's really the sort we should have in our own firm, and I'm sorry now that I didn't hire him on the spot."

Outside, I adjusted my muffler and pulled down my hat against the wind. The Weather Service had forecast up to ten inches of snow, and, sure enough, it was beginning to fall, but at the moment it drifted down softly, like confetti, which was the kind of snowfall I had always enjoyed walking in, imagining that the city was a place where magical things could happen, where life as well as the streets could take on a clean, new look.

Waiting on the corner, I put my paperbacks into my portfolio next to the gun, which I was dying to hold in my hand again. Already I was beginning to regard it as part of my basic equipment, like my keys, wallet, comb and ballpoint pen. I had read somewhere that Englishmen are born a whiskey behind. Maybe there were people who were born a gun behind, and needed only that to put them in step on the highway to success. I doubted that Dr. Stevenson had included that thought in his book. Writing for a general audience, he wouldn't have dared to.

Also in my possession was my copy of the *Times*, whose want ads it was my intention to study at Burger King. A BMW made a sudden swerve, almost hitting me as I crossed the avenue, and with a gun under my arm I didn't think twice about turning and shaking a fist at the driver, an executive-type who thought he had the right to run over workingmen just as lords of the manor used to have the right to ravish virgins. I had been surprised to learn in a lecture at the main branch of the Brooklyn Public Library that the great and pious Count Leo Tolstoy, the author of *War and Peace*, used to take advantage of the peasant girls on his vast estate in Russia.

"You son of a bitch!" I was surprised to hear myself saying to the driver. He glared at me a moment, and moved a hand toward the door as if he intended to come out and teach me my place in society. It was a good thing for his family that he didn't, for at that moment I was just angry enough to shoot him. I squared my shoulders and walked on. "Gesundheit!" I said to a woman with a sneezing fit. This gesture of goodwill was a proof that my animosity was only toward the unjust. An old nun with a black shawl over her head and shoulders and a raffia basket on her lap was sitting on a crate in a recessed doorway. The crate, something I hadn't seen since childhood, and mostly in Jewish neighborhoods, had once contained siphons of Good Health seltzer. I paused and dropped in a quarter.

"Aren't you cold, Sister?" I asked.

She didn't answer. Her watery gray eyes were open, and she was so still that I was afraid she had frozen to death, which would have been bad publicity for the Catholic Church, but I supposed they would have survived that as they had survived other embarrassments over the centuries.

"Are you okay?"

Finally her hands appeared from under her habit with a rosary, and she gave a faint smile which suggested to me that we had met before though I could not remember where or when. Decades ago, was she the friendly nun who used to care for the pathetic little garden across the street from St. Edmund's Church on Ocean Avenue? There had been a small statue of St. Fiacre, the saint devoted to gardens and also to the relief of hemorrhoids and VD.

"Oh," I said, understanding now that she had wanted to finish her prayer. "Sorry to disturb you. Just checking that everything's okay. Can I get you some hot tea or coffee?"

She shook her head emphatically, as if I had suggested a double vodka to a guy on the wagon. "God bless you," she murmured.

"Thanks. I'll be needing that. Today especially." I waved goodbye and proceeded to Burger King, hoping that the sister's dedication to the church in twenty-degree weather would get her right into heaven, and that God was more fair to His employees than any of my bosses had ever been.

On my first job I had worked on Kings Highway in a fruit and vegetable store after school and on weekends. Among other chores, I was supposed to weigh the side-walk merchandise for customers, mark the prices on the paper bags, and tell them to go inside to pay the owner's wife, who guarded the cash register as if it contained all the gold in Fort Knox.

"Never take the cash yourself," Mr. Seminara had warned me. "Tell them to pay my missus. Cash is *her* function. *Capice?*"

His order seemed simple enough, and I said, "Sure, Mr. Seminara."

A few days later I weighed out four pounds of pota-toes for a woman with a crying baby in a carriage. When she handed me a quarter I shook my head.

"Please pay inside."

"I no gotta da time. You tink maybe I got a hundred servants like the queen of England? My baby is crying to be changed and I gotta get home and make supper. Such formality! Like dinner at the White House when ambassadors come to call."

"It's the boss's strict rule."

"He's your boss, not mine. And you know what you are? You're a dumb jerk. And you can keep the penny change."

She pressed the quarter into my hand and rushed away. I turned to bring the quarter inside, but then another customer grabbed my sleeve and demanded to be served at once. She practically pulled me over to the bushel of string beans. "These better be fresh," she said. "I have to make a special Hungarian dish for my mother-in-law. Years ago I should have taken my own mother's advice and married an orphan."

I started to serve her, but then saw the boss running out of the store toward me.

"I saw you!" he screamed. "I saw you with my own eyes!"

"Saw what?"

"Don't act cute with me. I saw that customer pay you." He pulled open my hand, snatched the quarter, and held it up in triumph like it was a gold medal at the Olympics. "You were going to keep it!"

"I wasn't. The lady didn't have time to bring it inside."

"You should have told her it was my strict rule." He pounded his chest like a gorilla in a jungle movie. And his face got so red I thought he would have a heart attack, which I felt two ways about.

"I did tell her. I swear to God. But she didn't care."

"You're lying. You're a thief. You're a disappointment to me. I thought you were an honest Italian boy. Maybe you're not even Italian at all. I've always suspected that you were really a Yid like that guy who used to run the protection racket here on Kings Highway. Do you know what happens to thieves?"

"I'm no thief."

"You're fired! Fired! I don't want you here no more! If I ever see you on the block I'll call the cops."

"Fuck you, Mr. Seminara. Fuck you and your lousy job. I quit."

"You're going to end up in Sing Sing one day. In the electric chair."

The memory of that day about thirty-seven years ago still made my chest thump. Mr. Seminara no longer had the store on Kings Highway, but last summer I had seen him and a woman entering a pizza restaurant on Avenue L. I now imagined myself entering his apartment and confronting him with my gun.

"Hi, Mr. Seminara."

"Why are you pointing that gun at me?"

"I have to point it somewhere," I would say cleverly while he sweated and squirmed.

"Who are you?"

"Don't you remember me, Mr. Seminara? Think hard. Think back to thirty-seven years ago."

"You can't be!"

"Yes, I used to be just little George Mancuso, but now I'm Big George Mancuso, and Big Nick's most valued triggerman. But this isn't a professional job for Big Nick. This is a score of my own I want to settle."

"Don't. Please don't shoot me. I'm an old man and the short time I have left is precious to me. Spare me and I'll give you my supermarket up on Lexington Avenue. It does a net business of a million dollars a year. Beverly Sills and all the celebrities get their gourmet items there. I supply the new sushi restaurant that Barbara Walters loves better than any joint along the Ginza in Tokyo."

The scene was so vivid and satisfying that I played it over and over, and inside Burger King I walked into a man carrying a loaded tray. Luckily, I was wearing the expression for killing Mr. Seminara, and the other patron, instead of becoming abusive, just scowled and hurried away from me.

I carried my coffee to an empty table near the wall, and there I took out my *Times* and opened it to the want ads. I wished I were an accountant, because every firm in town seemed to be wanting one. Or that I were a dental technician or receptionist, or industrial engineer or word processor. There were only six ads for mail room jobs. For the best of them, a mail room supervisor with a worldwide retail organization and paying $13,500 a year, you were required to submit your resumé to a *Times* box number, and unfortunately I didn't have a resumé with me. Three of the others, however, listed a phone number, and I had nothing to lose by calling them. I finished my coffee and left Burger King to scout around for a bar with a phone.

Halfway up the block I passed Maxwell's, the rare-book store where I had answered a *Times* want ad immediately after finishing high school, by which time my mother had already been in a mental hospital for two years. The man who interviewed me said that there were other applicants for the job of general assistant, and that I would hear from him in a week or so.

By the time I finally did hear from him, the following month, to say that I could have the job (I was sure his first choice hadn't made the grade), I had already landed the mail clerk job at the *Globe* in response to another ad. I wondered what I would be like today if I had switched to Maxwell's. If only as an escape from my personal problems, I had always enjoyed reading all kinds of books, and would probably have taken to the work like a duck to water. And I would have had more incentive to attend college at night. By now, I would probably have been a well-paid and respected expert in rare books instead of an unemployed mail clerk whose next job would probably be for Big Nick.

A collector would rush up to me with an old book

and ask excitedly: "Mr. Mancuso, do you think this is a first edition of *A Tale of Two Cities*?"

I would reply patiently in the manner of an expert who must consider more factors than a mere layman could possibly imagine: "I really cannot tell you off the top of my head, so to speak. Please allow me to examine it first. Miss Smith, may I have my new magnifying glass, if you please.... Thank you, dear. Yes...Hm...Yes...No.... This marking on the title page disturbs me a bit. And there's also this foreword to the reader. As we experts know, Dickens did not start writing forewords until he published *David Copperfield* two years later. I'm sorry to disappoint you, Mrs. Stevens, but in my opinion this is a second edition at best, and not a very good copy at that."

Curious, I turned around and walked back to the bookstore and entered. The atmosphere was more that of a library than a place of business. Against a wall completely covered with shelves of books, wearing a white shirt, tie and blue jacket, a man of about my own age was sitting behind a desk. When his phone rang, he picked it up and smiled. He raised a hand casually and a beautiful young secretary appeared with a notebook. She wrote down what he dictated and then she walked off while he enjoyed his rear view of her, as men will do with their secretaries and other female personnel. He continued talking, obviously enjoying his phone conversation with a customer, perhaps a celebrity like Walter Cronkite who was researching his next bestseller. Occasionally he toyed with his necktie.

He picked up his pipe and a tobacco pouch. Suddenly he spotted me near the door, and after waving to me, ordered a young clerk in a tweed jacket, arranging books on a shelf, to wait on me.

"Good morning, sir," the clerk said, smiling. "May I help you?"

I wanted to tell him to work hard at his job, and then maybe in thirty years he'd have the soft and dignified position of his superior at the desk. But what I said was, "Upon second thought, I really haven't that much time to shop for a set of Shakespeare today."

"Well, any time you do, I'll be happy to help you. We have an excellent selection of the Bard, including the Globe edition."

"It's good to know that, but I won't be wanting the Globe edition."

He nodded his head in agreement that the Globe edition was not for a connoisseur like me. Next he ran forward and opened the door for me as politely as if I had just bought the complete works of Rudyard Kipling. And in genuine morocco binding.

Resuming my search for a bar with a telephone, I saw myself entering the Globe Building on that fateful day which would change my life forever. Ben, the elevator starter, whose name I didn't yet know, stood in the lobby between the two banks of elevators. Lean, in a gray uniform, with narrow eyes and a beaky nose, and holding a clicker, he sniffed at me and said sharply:

"Where you goin', kid?"

"I have an appointment with Mr. Warren of the *Globe*."

"The mail boy job?"

I preferred the want ad title of mail *clerk*. "Yes," I whispered.

"Room 610," he said with the air of a man who knew everything worth knowing.

"Thanks."

"Good luck, kid."

With the speed of a much younger man he ran across the lobby to assist a well-dressed man, obviously an important tenant, with a package. The last time I saw Ben, about fifteen years ago, was at Syms clothing store on Trinity Place, where we were both taking advantage of their great sale called The Bash. He had had a leg removed because of diabetes, and he walked with a crutch.

Carl drove me up in the elevator for *Globe* employees. His dark hair was thick and shiny, and his warm smile reminded me of James Garner the movie star.

"Six, please."

"The mail boy job?"

"Yes."

"Hope you get it, kid. Lots of good pussy at the *Globe*. Look out especially for Rita in the cashier's office." With his free hand he drew a semicircle over his chest. Upon second thought, he drew a larger semicircle. "Ain't kidding. You'll see for yourself."

"Can't wait," I said, one macho guy to another.

In the years to come I would think over and over about my first meeting with Mr. Warren. My appointment with him was for ten but I wasn't admitted into his office till exactly ten-fifty, and, like at a doctor's office, he didn't bother to apologize for having kept me waiting. He was tall, dark-haired and clean shaven, and quite heavy, and younger than I had expected him to be. Thirty-five, tops. He lit a king-size cigarette, waved me into a chair, and picked up the job application I had mailed in the week before.

His voice was deep, warm, and as smooth as honey, which should have been a warning to me, but I was young and innocent to the ways of business. "Okay," he said, "let's see what we have here." He slipped on a pair of dark-framed eyeglasses that made him look older and extremely efficient, an executive worthy of being pictured with Aristotle Onassis on the *Globe's* financial pages. While lowering his hands to my application, he discreetly picked his nose with a pinky. He made a buzzing sound through his nose that I first thought was a bee in the room.

"Are you by any chance related to Joe Mancuso in our subscription department? He's a good man. A regular churchgoer."

"No, sir. I mean, I'm not related to him. But I also go to church regularly."

"Good. Good. I see you live in Brooklyn."

"Yes, sir."

"A lot of famous Americans emanate from that neck of the woods."

"I know that." The first ones that came to my mind were the Gallo Brothers, who were associated with the Profaci crime family. But this didn't seem the right time and place to mention them. I mentioned instead Rita Hayworth, Susan Hayward and Mae West.

He addressed a stern look at me as he said, "Ever been arrested?"

"No, sir," I said, and shook my head.

He nodded his approval of my good conduct. And he returned to my application. "I suppose you live with your folks."

"No, sir."

He looked up from my application again. And tensed his brow.

"My father's dead. My mother's in a mental hospital."

"Sorry to hear that." He sighed. "Things have a way of happening."

"They certainly do. I live with an aunt and uncle."

"Is your mother coming along?"

"I don't think so. She's only gotten worse in the hospital."

"Which hospital is that?"

"Manhattan State."

"What's wrong with her exactly?"

I felt uncomfortable discussing my mother's condition, but I had to answer him. "Mostly, she has delusions.

She thinks my father is still alive. She cries all the time. She's tried to kill herself a few times."

"I'm sure science will come up with a cure one of these days. Some terrific new drug or advanced form of psychoanalysis. Take my word for it. I see you attended James Madison High School. I've heard some good things about it. Joe Goldstein, one of our sports reporters, went there."

"I know. He once addressed our journalism club."

"I see here that you belonged to that."

"Yes, sir. I also wrote some sports stories for our school newspaper."

"That's how some of our greatest reporters started out."

"I know that."

"I guess that's what you'd eventually like to be at the *Globe*."

"I'd like to try to be that, sir."

"Do you read Chet Haines's column?"

"Yes, sir."

"He also started in the mail room, and so did some of our other top-flight reporters. From three to six months in the mail room, and then transfer to the city room as copyboy, and from there"—Mr. Warren stretched out both arms to the side—"from there it's all according to your will and determination and talent."

"Yes, sir."

"'Cherish your visions and your dreams as they are

the children of your soul, the blueprints of your ultimate achievements.' That was said by Napoleon Hill, one of my favorite philosophers. To be candid, I learned more from him than those Greeks I had to study at Cornell."

My head was swimming with visions of myself as a reporter, whether of sports or general news. I was sure that the psychiatrists at Manhattan State were not trying very hard to cure my mother, and I would write an exposé that would lead to better treatment for all patients. I expressed this hope to Mr. Warren.

"I think that's a terrific ambition, George. If I may inquire," he continued, "why haven't you pursued your academic career and gone on to college? You look like a bright-enough lad for that, and since the days of the Founding Fathers, higher education has always been the stepping stone to success. I'm thinking especially of Abraham Lincoln, who was born in a log cabin and, rain or shine, had to trudge back and forth for miles to a little red schoolhouse."

Again I was embarrassed to discuss personal matters with a stranger. Aware of my reticence, Mr. Warren encouraged me with a smile. After lighting another cigarette, he slouched back in his chair and threw a leg across his desk.

"My mother went into the hospital while I was in my second term of high school. I went to live with my aunt and uncle, but they couldn't support me and I had to work after school and on holidays and weekends. They were nice and kind enough to see me through high school, and when I was finished I felt it my responsibility to get a full-time job right away."

"There's always night school. Some of our greatest journalists as well as leaders of industry and statesmen have taken that particular route to success. Ed Hirschhorn, our financial editor, for instance."

"I've heard of him. This semester I couldn't attend night school because of my job-hunting and everything, but I certainly intend applying in the future. I want to make something of myself and of my life," I said, remembering my father on his deathbed.

Mr. Warren nodded approval, and then he straightened up and leaned forward across his desk, looking so solemn that I thought he was going to tell me of his own misfortunes.

"True," he said, turning out his hand, "the mail room may not strike some people at first as a particularly important department, but in my opinion it is an absolutely indispensable one."

I hoped I looked equally solemn as he went on to tell me the functions of a mail room, about how mail was picked up early in the morning and at later hours too at the post office, about how it had to be sorted accurately, how it had to be delivered with dispatch not only to Mr. Drew, the publisher, and to all the other important executives and editors but to all the departments in the building. It was also the function of the mail room to pick up outgoing mail, stamp it by hand or machine with the proper postage, and deliver it several times a day to the post office. There was also the picking up of the various editions of the *Globe* in the pressroom and then their distribution throughout the building, making sure that Mr. Drew and the other VIPs got their papers first and in perfect condition. One of Mr. Drew's ancestors had been a lady-in-waiting to Queen Victoria of England, and she had passed down a family tradition of perfection in cleanliness and punctuality. There were also occasional errands to addresses off the premises.

"Do you think you're the man for all of that?" Mr. Warren asked afterward. "Lots of fellows have thought it would be a cinch. But they learned differently, and usually very soon. It will be a responsibility and a challenge." His pinky went up to his nose again. "It's a sometimes hard experience, but a most valuable one, I believe." He gave a little laugh. "Being only four, my son is not quite ready for the business world, but when he is, I could do worse than suggest that he begin in the mail room here at the *Globe*."

To prove that he was not exaggerating, or at least that he had a son, he turned round the photograph on his desk of a heavy brunette sitting on a piano stool between a boy and a girl. They all looked radiantly happy, and I didn't blame them, because Mr. Warren probably made a fantastic salary and could give them everything their hearts desired.

"They're all very beautiful," I said. "Your wife looks

like a younger Susan Hayward," I added, maybe putting it on a little. Anyhow, she looked more like Susan Hayward than like Barbara Stanwyck or Maureen O'Hara. "Around the nose and chin, especially."

He picked up the picture and examined it. "I see what you mean, George. You're a keen observer, which is a prime requisite for a journalist. I'm going to tell Bernice what you said. I think she'll be very pleased. Susan Hayward happens to be her favorite actress of all time. Years ago Bernice saw *I Want to Live!*, and she was positively shattered when Susan was convicted and sent to the chair."

"I can imagine."

He set down the picture and draped an arm over the back of his chair. With his other hand he stroked his chin while he studied my application in the way I had seen a doctor study my X ray in the emergency room of Coney Island Hospital after I hurt my ankle in a softball game.

"The pay will be fifty-two dollars a week to start, but there will be an increase after six months and another after a year." He looked at me inquiringly, as if probing my sense of values.

I was currently earning only forty dollars as a stock boy in a drug-supply house, and fifty-two sounded like a fortune.

"Sounds fine."

He lit another cigarette. He sucked in his lips and tapped his thighs. He took a deep breath. He hummed through his nose. He drummed his fingers against his desk.

"Decisions, decisions," he said.

I tried to look sympathetic over his executive dilemma. My stomach was churning. I hoped that I wouldn't have to go to the bathroom.

"Naturally, I've had quite a few other applicants for this desirable position." He scratched his head. He sighed. "But...but I kind of have a good feeling about you, George."

"Thank you, Mr. Warren."

He planted his elbows on his desk and laced his fingers together. He placed his chin on his fingers and scrutinized me a long time, and finally he leaned forward and extended a hand, saying, "Welcome aboard, George."

I had once heard the expression used by Noel Coward in an English movie about the royal navy, and I thought that Mr. Warren was incredibly sophisticated. His decision made me feel like an actor who had won the Academy Award. Feeling as light as air, I rose to my feet. "Thanks, Mr. Warren." I rushed forward to shake his hand. I promised to live up to his faith in me. He gave me directions to the mail room and told me to tell Al Vann, the department head, that he had sent me along....

Now, thirty-two years later, on Fifty-ninth Street, the snow began to fall harder and stick to the ground. I had put on my Florsheim shoes for the trip to the Plaza Hotel, and I hoped that the snow wouldn't rise high enough to damage them. On Third Avenue I turned north and after a few blocks came to an Irish bar and grill at whose downtown branch I often used to order the luncheon special while I was still at the *Globe.* Inside, I walked past the bar and food section, hoping to find a telephone booth in the rear. I was astounded by the prices of their sandwiches, corned beef costing five dollars. Back when I'd started at the *Globe,* their sandwiches had been mostly in the dollar-fifty-cent range. The huge roast beefs and fatty corned beefs on the steam table always disturbed me, because they reminded me of the animals from which they were cut, and many was the time I had resolved to become a vegetarian like my friend Phil Levinson, though I never did. Vegetarians were supposed to be healthier and live longer, but Phil eventually came down with colitis and was forbidden to eat some of his favorite whole grains and fruits and vegetables. Go figure.

Though it was not yet noon, there were already men and even a few women at the bar. I knew from reading the newspapers that a lot of rub-outs were done in bars like this, and I imagined that I was already in Big Nick's employ and he had assigned me to process the man in the brown overcoat staring down at his shot glass. He looked deep in thought, and was probably an advertising man planning a campaign for toothpaste or tuna fish. Little did he know that the toothpaste and tuna would have to find their way to consumers without him. After shooting him, I would order the bartender and patrons to lie down on the floor.

"Okay, I don't want to hurt anyone else unless I have to. You too, miss, you too have to get down. I'm sorry if your coat gets soiled. Better to spend a few dollars at the cleaner's than a few thousand for a funeral. Am I right or am I wrong? I'm leaving now. Stay down for the count of a hundred. It doesn't pay to be a dead hero. So what if your name gets mentioned in the *News* or the *Globe*?"

A redhead of about forty was standing at the phone attached to the wall. While I didn't wish to eavesdrop on her conversation, I felt I should stand within a few feet of her so that other users would know that I was next in line. Discreetly, I looked down at my newspaper.

"Frederick, Frederick!" she was saying. "Are you listening to me? I don't care what's happened in the past. The question now is, Where do we go from here? I think you could have told me about Veronica. I'm a big girl. I would have understood. I never for a moment dreamed I was the first woman in your life. Hold on for a second." She turned to me, fluttered her long and phony eyelashes, and said, "I'd be ever so obliged for change of a dollar."

"I beg your pardon?" I said, pretending like a gentleman that I hadn't been aware of her presence and conversation on the phone.

"I'd appreciate change of a dollar."

Her aggressive smile made me wonder if she'd been a model in younger days. I felt in my pockets, came across larger coins, but felt I needed them for my own calls. "I'm sorry, but I can lend you a quarter in change if it'll help."

Suddenly she had an English accent: "It would help me tremendously. You're very, very kind."

"Don't mention it."

She dropped in a coin and said, "Okay, you greedy robot, there's your filthy lucre.... Where were we?... I beg your pardon, you creep! What business is it of yours whom I'm with? You didn't tell me about Veronica until after three months, by which time you'd taken everything a woman has to offer.... Okay, I *will* tell you." The red-head smiled and nodded to me over her shoulder. "I'm with someone who's warm and kind and is, above all, a gentleman.... What difference does it make what he looks like?... Okay, his hair is brown with a certain amount of gray that makes him look very distinguished. He's broad and strong and looks like a younger Charlton Heston but much better dressed than in all those movies that take place in ancient Rome or Egypt." She glanced at my portfolio. "And he's quite a successful businessman.... No, he's not Murray Feldenchrist. Look, you could guess all day and all night and you still wouldn't know who he is.... Yes, it is definitely possible that he's from abroad. Possibly from England. And an ancestral estate in Surrey.... No, he is not gay. Far from it, in fact."

Feeling very uncomfortable about my involvement in this romantic crisis, I walked over to the bar and ordered a beer that I didn't really want or need. I sat there until

I saw the redhead hang up the phone, and then I rushed forward before a newcomer could snatch it. We passed each other without a word or a look. I supposed that Big Nick often got orders to knock off guys like Frederick who had two-timed their mistresses.

"Are you Frederick?"

"Yes, and who are you?"

"That's unimportant."

"What are you doing with that gun?"

"Sorry, pal, only doing my job."

"Elizabeth hired you, didn't she? I can explain about Veronica. I met her at a cocktail party and it became one of those mad, mad passions like in a novel by Danielle Steel. But I swear to you by all that's holy that it was never anything serious between us. My heart always belonged to Elizabeth. From the moment I saw her red hair, I knew she was the one woman for me. You must believe that. How much is she paying you? I'll pay you double and throw in my Buick Electra in the bargain. It's practically new, with less than ten thousand miles."

I dropped a quarter into the slot and dialed the prestigious midtown home furnishings company that was looking for a bright individual who was familiar with postage rates and regulations, which was me, I hoped.

"Mr. Ortenga, please."

"Is this in reference to the mail room position?" a woman asked.

"Yes, ma'am."

"The position's been filled. Thanks for calling." She hung up.

I cursed myself for having gone to Mr. Anthony at the Plaza when I should have been studying the want ads. I lit a cigarette before dialing the next number.

"Mr. Sorenson, please."

"Is this in reference to the mail room position?" a woman asked again, and I wondered if it was the same one as before.

"Yes, it is, miss," I said, oozing both charm and competence. Or so I hoped.

"It may be filled by now, but I'll put you through."

"Thank you, miss." I hoped that my manners would so impress her that she would tell Mr. Sorenson that a particularly attractive prospect was available.

"Hello," Mr. Sorenson growled.

"Good morning." I was sorry I hadn't looked into the Suzy Christopher book while at the bar, but I hoped that her smiling picture now before me on the cover would offer inspiration. "I'm very much interested in the position in today's *Times*."

"Aren't you waking up a little late? I've already had a lot of applicants. However...what's your name?"

"George Mancuso."

"You're Italian."

"Yes, and so were all the popes until recently."

"You seem to have a sense of humor, Mr. Mancuso."

"I try to look at the bright side when at all possible."

"Positive thinking certainly never hurt a man, especially in the shoe business. That's what we do here, distribute shoes that we import from some of the finest manufacturers all over the globe."

"Oh," I said, trying to sound fascinated. I decided not to try a little humor and remark that I wore shoes all the time.

"How old are you?"

At first I had an urge to lie and say forty-one, but then I told the truth, and added, "Fifty is the prime of life, and I've had a lot of experience in mail rooms."

"How many exactly? I hope you're not a job-hopper."

"Oh, no, sir. To tell the truth, I'm a very steady employee. All my experience was in the mail room of the *Globe*."

"Globe Better Footwear over on Fifth and Forty-third? It's a wonder to me how they stay in business."

"No. The *New York Globe*. The newspaper, you know."

He grunted. "Never read it. It's a filthy, commie rag."

"That's a new one on me. As a matter of fact, its publisher, Randolph T. Drew, and J. Edgar Hoover once belonged to the same country club and went to horse races together. Anyhow, I wasn't responsible for their news or editorials, only for my duties in the mail room."

"How long were you there?"

"Over thirty years."

"That's quite a long time."

Too long, I said to myself. *Too long.* The thought of all those years gone down the drain made my eyes tickle, and I was afraid I was going to cry. After a deep breath I told Sorenson, "I like to think of myself as a steady man."

"You sound hoarse. Do you have a cold? Is your health up to par?"

"My health is fine. I'm in the prime of life, as they say. I'm in shape to tackle a longshoreman's job, but my primary interest is in mail rooms."

"They're certainly an indispensable department in any organization."

"I know that better than anyone."

"Were you the head of the mail room at the *Globe*?"

"In recent years, I'd worked my way up to assistant head."

"I see. Who was your supervisor?"

"My top supervisor was Mr. John C. Warren, but my immediate one for a long time was Al Vann, and when he quit a few months ago and was replaced by a newcomer named Pat Merman, a girl who had never—"

"Was that a woman? Am I hearing correctly?"

"Yes, sir."

"I was not aware that any firms in town had women in the mail room."

"Well, the *Globe* wanted one."

"If I may ask, why did she get the position over you with all your experience? Did they think you lacking in supervisory capability?"

Tears were falling from my eyes by now, and I wished that Sorenson would stop harping on the present subject.

"I don't think the *Globe* had any dissatisfaction with my supervisory capability. While Al Vann was on vacation or out sick, I was invariably the acting head of the mail room."

"Why did you leave the *Globe*? Were you dismissed?"

"I was not dismissed. I resigned."

"Why did you resign after thirty years of service?"

"I resigned for personal reasons."

"Was it your health? Do you have a drinking problem?"

"My health is fine, as I've already mentioned. And I don't recall ever being drunk in my life."

"You don't have to raise your voice."

At this point I was ready to slam down the phone, but I desperately wanted a legit job, and so I swallowed my pride, or what was left of it. "I'm sorry, sir. I didn't realize I was raising it. I've always been proud of my moderate drinking habits."

"What do you call moderate?"

"Maybe a glass of wine before dinner."

"I see. Well, frankly, Mr. Mancuso, I think that we're really looking for a rather younger man, someone recently out of school."

"You say in your ad that you want someone with supervisory experience. A kid fresh out of school wouldn't have that."

"Yes, but I think that, all in all, it would be more desirable. Thanks for calling us."

I couldn't help shouting, "If you don't know what you really want, why did you put in that particular ad?"

"Let's not lose our cool, Mr. Mancuso."

"I think you're discriminating against mature men and are therefore breaking the law of this state. I think you're a son of a bitch and I wouldn't take your lousy job even it if was offered to me."

"That's hardly likely after your outburst."

"Go to hell, Mr. Sorenson. And I hope your company goes bankrupt. Or the government slaps a big tariff on your fucken shoes that are probably made of cheap plastic and by prison labor in China."

I slammed down the phone. I wiped my eyes with a tissue. My heart was beating so fast that I was afraid I was coming down with a heart attack. Seeing the bump of the gun in my portfolio, I imagined myself in Sorenson's office, surprising him as he touched the breasts of the secretary who was sitting on his lap.

"Get out of here, miss. This is strictly between me and your boss."

As she ran out of the office, I knew she wouldn't re-port me to the cops. A widow with two children, she had allowed him to take liberties with her body only because she wanted to keep her job, and now she was secretly glad that this sexual harasser was about to get his due.

"Please don't do it, Mr. Mancuso. The job is still

yours if you want it. Now that I see you in person, I can tell you have the makings of a top-notch shoe executive, perhaps even another Cecil B. Florsheim. Let me show you around the executive suite so that you can pick out an office. Do you have a preference in desks and carpets? I strongly recommend—"

He was destined never to finish his sentence. My bullet hit him right in the heart, exactly where I had aimed it. I bent over his body to make sure he was dead, and then hurried to the door and wiped my fingerprints from the knob with the large white handkerchief that I always carried for that purpose. Outside, his secretary was sitting at her desk.

"I'm sorry you had to be present, miss."

"That's okay. It couldn't have happened to a more indecent executive. Too bad that the New York State Department of Sexual Harassment never responded to any of my complaints over the years."

She wanted to thank me profusely, but I really had no time to dally, and so I waved goodbye and stuck my gun into my belt.

I had been oblivious of the redhead during my conversation with Sorenson, but she had been standing nearby, and she handed me a quarter as she said, "That's telling off the son of a bitch."

"He had it coming to him."

"He sure did. He's a bastard. The world is full of them."

"You can say that again."

"You're still shaking. Let me buy you a brandy."

"No, thank you."

"In that case, you can buy me one."

Before I could think of a polite way of saying that I'd rather not, she was already over at the bar and waving to the bartender. Rather than create an awkward situation, I put my portfolio under my arm and followed her.

"A Hennessy, Paul."

When Paul smiled at me to convey that a real gent does not permit a lady to drink alone, I had to nod that I would have the same. I remembered that Mr. Warren always looked particularly pleased when he unwrapped a Christmas gift I had delivered and it turned out to be an expensive brandy such as Hennessy. Once, in an expansive mood, he said he would call me in for a drink when he opened a bottle on Christmas Eve. But he never did though he called in a lot of other people, including Al Vann.

"Cheers," the redhead said.

"Cheers," I responded, and after the brandy had burned my throat and I could speak again, I told her, "This is the earliest I've ever had a drink."

"Time is relative, Albert Einstein says."

"That's true, I suppose, but he's too deep for me."

"What time do you usually have your first drink of the day?"

"If I have one at all, it's at about six-thirty, a glass of wine or a highball before my wife and I have dinner."

She looked at the slim gold watch on her wrist. "It's now eleven-ten here in New York. But I believe that in London or in Paris, it's exactly six-thirty. Make believe you're there."

"Okay," I said with a laugh. "I'll do that."

"Now what time is it?"

"It's six-thirty and I'm in Paris."

"*Oui, oui, monsieur.*"

"Are you French?"

She lit a Kool and said, fluttering her lashes, "Do I look French?"

As dim as it was, the light here was brighter than near the telephone in the back, and I saw that she was closer to fifty than forty, and that her hair was dark at the roots. Lines ran from her eyes and the ends of her mouth, and her eyes were pouchy and her throat was lined.

She popped the cigarette into her mouth and placed her hand between us at eye level. "Hey! That's not fair. A man doesn't look that closely at a girl except on Saturday night, when she's slapped on all her makeup and is wearing her best bra and perfume."

"Sorry." Because I'd awakened that morning with one of my stomach spasms, I had had only a slice of toast and a cup of weak tea for breakfast, and now I began to feel the brandy. "Well," I went on, "you certainly could be French. Your features remind me a little of the French movie actress Annabella, whom I saw on TV in *Suez* with Tyrone Power a few weeks ago."

"Thanks for the compliment. No, I'm not French, but I studied it in high school and visited Paris with Larry, my second husband, for a week in '73."

I nodded that this information was very interesting to me.

"My name is Cathy, by the way."

"Mine is George."

"One doesn't meet as many Georges as one used to."

I smiled. "Well, you're meeting one now."

"So I am."

"Cathy is a very nice name, I think. At the video store, my wife and I have taken out *Wuthering Heights*, in which Merle Oberon is Cathy."

"It's one of my favorites too." She chewed a thumb for a few moments and then said, "When *my* various Heathcliffs came along, none of them looked remotely like Laurence Olivier."

"I guess a good Heathcliff is hard to find."

My remark really broke her up. She had just swallowed the remains of her brandy, and she burst out laughing and coughing together. I leaned forward, coming so close that I could look down and see her substantial breasts, or maybe it was just her high-tech bra, the sort worn by Marlene Dietrich, or so I had once read somewhere. I didn't look down deliberately, but she caught me in the act, and gave a giggly laugh that I supposed was mostly the result of her brandy.

"You're really very witty," she said. "Are you sure

you're not Neil Simon incognito? When I was based in L.A., I dated one of the writers on the Bob Newhart show, and he never said anything near that witty."

"Thanks for the compliment. No, I'm not Neil Simon, though I wish I had his dough."

"Don't we all. You're not the only one beating the pavements, George. I've been three months without an assignment."

"What do you do?"

"Wouldn't you like to know?" She fluttered her eyelashes. "But seriously...right now I'm ready to take anything I can get, but I'm really an actress. I used to be a model also." She ran a hand down her hip and buttock.

"I'm sure you could still be a model."

"No, I've run to fat in my old age. Or maybe it's cellulite. I've always been confused about the difference. Do you mind if I have another brandy?" she asked, already signaling the bartender.

"Be my guest," I said graciously, and as if I had a choice. "Make it two, Paul," I told the bartender, and patted my pocket to make sure that I still had my wallet. About a week ago, Larry King's guest on CNN was a reformed pickpocket, and he had revealed the three best areas in town for his former profession, and I was in one of them.

"And make mine a double." Cathy pressed her palms together like a good little girl who deserves a treat. She watched fascinated while Paul poured, and then she took a hearty gulp, hopped off her stool, slipped off her coat, and extended her arms in a model's posture.

"You may remember me from the *Big Bonanza* show on NBC in the mid-sixties. I was Gloria, sort of a hostess, and when Flip Fisher revealed the prizes of the studio participants who had guessed the right answers, dressed in my leotards I would shake my fanny and boobs as I leaned over and pointed to the prizes, whether an RCA stereo or a Pontiac hardtop."

Cathy proceeded to bend and shake as she pointed to imaginary prizes, speaking with the happy, breathless voice of Flip Fisher, who had recently jumped to his death from a Las Vegas hotel room after being unable to find work worthy of his former celebrity. "But wait! There's more for you, Estelle and William Smithers of Adams, Nebraska, which has always been one of my favorite towns in the nation! With the compliments of Westinghouse, makers of fine products for home and industry, you can take home this self-defrosting refrigerator with built in can opener, blender and coffee grinder. Never again will there be a need to prepare your own milk shakes, Estelle and William. At the turn of a dial and the press of a button, you open your Westinghouse and take out your milk shake in any of two dozen delicious flavors, including low-calorie raspberry fudge!"

Cathy went on to announce and demonstrate a couple of other prizes, but I soon tired of her performance and wished she would stop. She had worked herself into a frenzy and was beginning to remind me of a young black woman in my mother's ward who believed she was Althea Gibson, the tennis champ, and she would follow visitors around, demonstrating her various strokes.

By the time Cathy had finished she was gasping for breath, and she leaned against the bar looking as exulted as if she had just won the Emmy Award in her category.

"Terrific!" I said, clapping, and extended a glass of water.

She ignored the water and reached for her brandy, which she finished in a single gulp, afterward plopping down on her stool and sticking a cigarette into her mouth.

"You're a doll, George." She gave me a bright smile. "Do you know something? You're a doll."

Having looked in the mirror while shaving that morning, I could not believe that this was leading up to anything for either of us. Though she was sexually desirable, as are most women until you know them better and/ or see them undressed, I was a married man, and so I slipped off my stool, picked up my portfolio, and prepared to leave. But Cathy grabbed my hand.

"Where you going, George? We were just getting to know each other."

"At one o'clock I have a job interview all the way downtown."

"You have plenty of time. And the subway is only a minute away."

Beyond Cathy's head and the heads of other drinkers,

something seemed to be going on down at the other end of the bar. Paul was standing still and looking straight ahead, and soon, still holding his bar rag, he raised both hands. I turned a bit to my left and saw a man in a blue parka standing in front of Paul, and holding a gun on him. In a few seconds the man stepped back and turned to look across the length of the bar and the food area opposite.

"Quiet, everybody," he said. "In case you missed Al Pacino in *Dog Day Afternoon*, this is a stickup. Everybody cooperate and no one will get hurt."

Cooperate had been my least favorite word back at the *Globe*. Whenever Al Vann had an unpleasant job or shift for me, he would first say, knowing I had no choice, that he was seeking my cooperation. Maybe it was this bitter memory that made me think of the gun in my portfolio, and I reached for the tab and slowly pulled open the zipper. From where he was standing, I was sure the robber couldn't see what I was doing.

"All of you, take your wallets out! And take off your watches and jewelry! When I pass among you, have them ready and put them into my tote bag. As you can all tell from the logo, it's from Channel Thirteen, and you too can have one for the basic contribution of as little as fifty bucks or whatever. By the way, I'd advise you not to watch their Wall Street program with Louis Rukeyser on Friday nights. Last year I lost more than a grand on his fucken tips. Instead, if I'd won big, you and I wouldn't be in this situation today. That's the way life goes."

Through her alcoholic haze, Cathy became fully aware of what was going on, and she clamped a hand over her wristwatch and whispered to me, "It was a gift from Gerald. He was a captain in the army, and a staunch Republican, and died heroically in Vietnam. I've held on to it through thick and thin. I'd rather die than lose it."

"What's going on there?" the robber called out. Fanning the air with his gun, he started in our direction, walking faster and faster. He was in his late twenties, short, and as nervous as a pig at a barbecue, as Jed McIntosh, the *Globe*'s hunting and fishing columnist, would have said.

At the *Globe*, Tim MacGregor, a retired city cop, used to head the small squad of security guards, and on Thursdays and Fridays, payroll days, he used to be stationed near the cashier's office which was full of cash. His ambition, after retirement from New York's Finest, had been to own a stable of whores in his former precinct, where his old buddies believed in protecting their own. But somehow it hadn't worked out for reasons having mainly to do with a tough homicide detective with the exact same plans for *his* second career. I had once asked Tim, while waiting on line to cash my check, what was the best way to handle a criminal.

"Elementary, my dear George." Tim grinned as he drew the gun from his holster. "Make him shit scared of you. Let him know at once that you're the boss."

Cathy clutched my arm as the robber approached.

It's lucky that it was my right arm and that I'm a south-paw. With a speed that would have made Clint Eastwood envious, I pulled the gun from my portfolio and said in a cool, even voice while I aimed at his heart:

"Freeze, you fuckin' son of a bitch! Freeze! Drop that fuckin' gun or I'll drop you, you bastard." For good measure I added, "Boy! Will I cooperate with you, you creep bastard! I'll cooperate right to the cemetery. Do you have a preference? If you're Catholic, you can't do better than Calvary." Many, many years ago, according to their wishes, that's where the two lovebirds, Alice's Uncle James and Mildred, his Jewish wife, were buried together in his family grave. In the relevant paperwork for the cemetery, to avoid complications both spiritual and financial, her birth name was changed ever so slightly from Goldstein to Goldoni.

While he stared open-mouthed, the robber's body shook from head to toe. His hands trembled, and the gun and tote bag fell to the floor. I ran forward and with my free hand pushed him across the room against the wall and ordered him to turn round and spread-eagle.

"Anyone here know how to handle a gun?" I asked.

From his perch on a bar stool, a middle-aged man in a blue pin-stripe suit raised his hand. And he said, "I spent the happiest years of my life in the U.S. Marines, and used to shack up with a different dame every night. That was living, man. I would reenlist today if they would have me and I could figure out how to continue sending my kids to their Ivy League schools and also paying for my wife's shopping and losses at bridge. I love her as much as on our wedding day, but she is positively the worst bridge player in Westchester County and she hangs out with a crowd who are absolutely without mercy and wouldn't hesitate to bluff a world-class expert like Omar Sharif."

I picked up the robber's gun and handed it to the former Marine. "Keep the meatball covered," I snapped in the manner of Humphrey Bogart. "I have to go now."

"I'll call 911," the bartender said. "Stick around and get your name and picture in the papers. You're a fuckin' hero."

"No time," I said, turning toward the door.

Cathy grabbed her coat and ran after me. "Wait for me!"

"I'd like to show my appreciation," the bartender said. "Come back any time and have a drink on the house."

"I'll take one for him right now," said Cathy. "My usual."

"Be my guest," I said

I waited impatiently for Cathy to swallow her brandy. She followed me outside and up the street, a little wobbly on her high heels. I wanted to be far away by the time the cops arrived and asked questions about my gun.

"I'm really surprised, Cathy, that you still wear such high heels. Unless it's a social occasion, my wife and most of her friends now wear Reeboks or Easy Spirits."

"I was never more surprised. Where'd you get the gun, George?"

"I do a little private-eye work on the side."

"I knew you weren't really a mail room worker, that you were a man of action like John Wayne."

Pleased by the comparison, I said with a modest nod, "Things ain't always what they seem to be."

"They certainly ain't."

"It's snowing hard. Why don't you go home?"

She grabbed my sleeve and stopped, forcing me to stop too.

"I want to go home, but I don't want to go alone. Come with me, honey."

"I can't."

"Why can't you?"

I tapped my portfolio. "I'm on a case."

"It won't take long. I live just a few blocks from here. Just see me to my door. A gentleman always sees a lady to her door, and usually doesn't even have to be asked. Are you ashamed to be seen with me? Am I too old or ugly?"

"Of course it's not that. You're young and beautiful."

"Just to my door. I'm not feeling too steady on my feet." Sure enough, she began to sway.

"Okay," I said.

"It's just a few blocks."

She took my hand as if we were far from strangers. I wasn't sure where I was going exactly, but I was on my way.

On our way to her place, Cathy told me of her true love, who had been killed by a sniper in Vietnam, and whose body lay in a swamp for days until the area was liberated by his buddies. Her first marriage had been broken up by her mother-in-law, whose many complexes would have driven even Freud crazy. She stopped to gaze at the bottles in the window of a liquor store. And then she looked at me like when I used to shop at Key Foods with the kids and they wanted me to buy a new and expensive breakfast cereal.

"No," I said. "I think you drink too much."

"I drink as much as I have to. I'm all alone. You've got your wife to keep you level."

I was glad she remembered I had a wife.

After several blocks up Lexington Avenue, she crossed the street and turned the corner. Midway toward Third Avenue she paused at a small apartment building that was older and shabbier than any of the others we'd passed.

"Is this it?" I asked.

"Home is where they send you the rent bill."

I laughed and put out my hand. "It was certainly a pleasure to meet you, Cathy. Good luck in your life and career."

She grabbed my hand and pulled me toward the door. "See me upstairs like a proper gent."

"I really have to go now."

"I'm afraid to go upstairs alone."

"It's broad daylight."

"The hall light has been broken for over a week. A woman was recently raped and stabbed in the lobby. It was really gruesome. Naturally, the story made the front page of the *Post*. As for Page Six, in case you're interested, it had a few lines about Tony Curtis that day. He was taking piano lessons so that he could portray either Chopin or Schubert in a forthcoming movie. His choice would depend on a survey by his staff and outside advisers. He said that if he were an African-American like his friend Sidney Poitier, his strong preference would be Scott Joplin, which would give him a chance to extend his range and depict the poor guy's descent to madness."

She was telling the truth, at least about there being no light inside. We walked side by side upstairs to the second floor. The air was musty and the stairs squeaked and cracked like in a haunted house in the movies. On the landing she opened her purse and withdrew a key ring with a Rolls-Royce insignia.

"That's right, I'm a bit of a snob. And it cost the same in a thrift shop as a Ford or Fiat. Would you kindly oblige? I don't think I can quite manage it. That last brandy. You should have talked me out of it." She wagged a finger as if I had done something naughty.

Her door had three locks, which, to my knowledge, was more than the norm in Gravesend, my own part of Brooklyn. As I turned the third, she took my arm, opened the door, and pulled me inside.

"I'll make you a cup of coffee. Coffee is one of my few accomplishments. Even my former mother-in-law used to admit that."

She switched on a light and I saw we were in a narrow foyer. On a closet door was a Paris street scene by Maurice Utrillo, who, like Scott Joplin, had been no stranger to mental institutions. Years ago Alice and I had bought the same picture, but in a different frame, at Woolworth's for a few dollars. Over a bookcase stuffed with paperbacks were pictures of Julie Harris and Julie Andrews.

"Two of my idols," Cathy said. "Back at drama class in college, Miss Mowbray used to say that every aspiring actress should have idols to look up to."

A hairy blond dog of about the size of my cat at home came out of an open doorway and gave a weak little yelp.

"Meet Mitzi, my ferocious watchdog. She knows you're a nice guy or else she'd have been at your throat like a hungry lion."

"Hi, Mitzi. Nice to meet you."

She switched on another light. The living room was very small and very sloppy, with newspapers and magazines strewn on the dark corduroy sofa and cocktail table. The picture over the sofa, a Van Gogh reproduction, showed a peasant woman walking alone down a road extending far into the distance. Alice and I had seen the original at a show at the Brooklyn Museum many years ago. We had waited in line for an hour, but it had been worth it.

"Home, sweet home," Cathy said, slipping off her coat and throwing it on a chair.

"Very cozy."

"Forgive the mess. I wasn't expecting to bring home a reincarnation of Humphrey Bogart."

"You don't have to impress me, Cathy."

"I know I don't. You're not a phony. All the other men I've met in New York are phonies."

"Are you from out of town?"

"A suburb of Boston."

"Maybe you should go back."

"I've burned my bridges behind me." Suddenly she was behind me and pulling at my coat.

"I really have to go."

"Please stay a few minutes. I'm afraid to be alone. Maybe, being a man, you're never afraid...."

Lately, out of work and alone all day except for our cat, Rocky, I too had known times of fear, fear that Alice would never return home to me and I would be alone forever.

"Of course I'm sometimes afraid."

I was afraid now of something else, but I let her slip off my coat. She placed it over hers on the chair. Next she pointed to a corner near a lamp, where a sheet of paper stuck out of a typewriter upon a card table.

"Please don't look at that," she said. "I'm writing a novel."

"That's very interesting. What's it about?"

"It's about a sweet and innocent girl from a Boston suburb who learns the bitter truth about human relations. What else could it be about?"

"I look forward to reading it when it's published."

"*If* it's published. You can't imagine the conniving in the world of publishing. According to my podiatrist, who used to treat Gore Vidal and Truman Capote, it's every bit as bad as show biz." She walked over to the window and looked out. "It's still snowing."

"Maybe I should leave before transportation gets snarled."

"I feel we're in our own little oasis of peace and tranquility."

She sat down on the sofa and gestured me to sit down beside her. I sat down a little away from her, but she wiggled closer.

"Are you afraid of me, George?" She placed a hand on her breast. "Or maybe afraid of catching AIDS?"

"Of course not." I felt my temples throbbing. And I began to get an erection. And, now that she had mentioned it, to worry about AIDS.

She smiled tenderly, like a woman who shares her experience with Preparation H in a TV commercial. "Don't be afraid. More than ever these days, a woman can't rely upon male gallantry, and so I keep a supply of those unromantic little gadgets. What an age we're living in!"

I nodded to convey that she was acting wisely. And

by drawing away, I tried to suggest that her supply of condoms did not concern me.

She wiggled closer again, closer enough for me to feel her thigh and hip, and to worry about losing control and staining my shorts and trousers. "I'm sure that, with all their genius, even Shelley and Keats couldn't find anything romantic to write about AIDS and condoms. But Byron maybe, and Walt Whitman. Whitman most definitely. He would describe the perfect and shiny bodies of the workers in Malaya who grow the rubber for the condoms. Of course, one can never tell about Emily Dickinson. Everything is symbols with her. When she writes about a bird or a flower, she probably has a penis in mind." She shrugged a shoulder. "Maybe I just have a dirty mind." She fluttered her lashes. "By the way, do you find me attractive?"

In my youth, I could have never conceived of my ever resisting the advances of such an attractive woman, or of almost any woman at all. But I could not conceive of many things in those distant days. As I started to rise to my feet, she seized my hand and pressed it. And then she placed it on her thigh as she squinted across the room and said, "Do you believe in God and religion and all of that?"

"Sometimes."

"Sometimes." She shook her head, then closed her eyes a moment. "If we could only believe *all* of the time. I believe less and less of the time."

"Sorry to hear that. What's your religion, by the way?"

"I was raised Episcopalian."

I nodded as if I now understood something important about her.

"I went to a friend's funeral two weeks ago. We had started out in show biz together. In fact, we met at an audition for a play whose name I don't remember now. We didn't get the job and were later delighted that the play was a big flop and the producer went bankrupt and the author was sued for plagiarism and the director had to go back to Hollywood and resume making cheap horror movies for morons. Anyhow, my friend took an overdose, and I was one of the few at the very basic funeral service at the cemetery, where I saw her body being lowered into the ground. I looked down and saw ants crawling."

"You shouldn't have looked."

"I'm afraid, George. I'm afraid of dying."

"You're still young. Your best years are still ahead of you."

"I'm afraid of living too."

"We're all afraid sometimes."

"I'm cold. I'm starting to shiver."

"Maybe you should make that coffee now. Can I help you?"

"Hold me, please."

I thought of Alice typing away in her office. Or perhaps she was already out to lunch and eating her tuna sandwich and a cup of her current favorite flavor of yogurt, banana-strawberry. For a while her favorite flavor was boysenberry, but suddenly it was no longer being sold at Key Foods, our local supermarket. Or even at Finast, which was farther away but advertised itself as a super-su-permarket. Go figure.

My erection was at full mast now, but I still didn't think that matters would necessarily have to go all the way. At the last minute the telephone would ring. Or Cathy would decide to make up with Frederick, the guy she was phoning in the bar.

I put my arm around Cathy, and she put her head on my shoulder. She was silent for a while, and I began to hope that she had passed out from her brandy. But then I felt her hand touch mine. She squeezed it hard, and began to guide it along her thigh, across to her crotch, and then up past her belly to her breast, which was unfa-miliar and very different from Alice's. By this time, being a normal guy with normal instincts, I no longer needed any guidance from Cathy or her hand. My temples were throbbing, my heart was hammering, my lower parts were aching. I threw Cathy across my lap and clamped my lips against hers and pressed with all my might. With my hand I explored her breasts, her belly, her hips. As I reached for her vulva, she returned my hand to a breast and freed her mouth. Then, after a gasp and a moan, she said with a smile, "Please, not here, George. I'm not a kid anymore, and this position is breaking my back."

"Sorry."

"I forgive you. By the way, do you know of a good chiropractor?"

"He's way out in Brooklyn."

"Forget it."

With an arm round each other's waist, we left the living room. Cathy switched off the light as she informed me of her outrageous bills from Con Edison, and the number of its lobbyists in City Hall and Albany. We came to facing doors in the foyer. Cathy pointed to one of them.

"The bathroom, just in case."

"Thank you. A moment ago you mentioned you had something...."

She sighed. "And we once thought that the Pill would solve all of our sex problems. How young and foolish we were. I'll be back in a jiff."

As she opened the other door, I couldn't help noticing that her bed was unmade, which would have shocked Alice, who always arranged the pillows and spread as if she expected a photographer from *Good Housekeeping* to drop in. She returned in a few moments and casually handed me the red packet as if it were a sample of a new cookie or candy being offered outside a movie theater or department store. "Give me about five minutes," she murmured. "Be seeing you, honey."

In the bathroom, I saw on the hamper a bottle of the

same brand of color rinse that Alice used, Clairol Loving Care, and I quickly looked away from it, and also from the mirror.

After exactly seven minutes I stepped out and knocked at her door.

"*Entrez, mon cher,* but please close the door after you. Mitzi has a tendency to voyeurism."

I waved to Mitzi standing in the foyer and entered. The venetians were down and closed. The room smelled like one of those perfume departments where I looked for gifts for Alice, usually settling for an old favorite instead of something new and daring, which might arouse great expectations that I couldn't satisfy.

"Don't turn on the light," Cathy whispered from the bed, which I was relieved to see was a double, because Alice and I had once passed an uncomfortable night in a relative's single bed out on Fire Island, of all places, where I would have expected beds big enough for a mass orgy. "You can put your things on that chair."

I still couldn't believe what I was doing. I tried to look and feel sophisticated, but my fingers shook as I took off my tie and unbuttoned my shirt. I heard a click and then the sort of hopefully soothing music that's played in a dentist's office.

"Irving Berlin may be a fine song writer," Cathy said, "but I hear from the grapevine that he was not the nicest person in the world."

"Surprising. One would have thought from his music

that he was a great guy as well as a greater patriot than Robert Dole and Ronald Reagan combined."

"Wouldn't one."

I almost lost my balance and fell as I removed my shorts, and I was glad I was wearing a new pair of Fruit of the Looms. I had worn an older pair on the night I suffered a kidney stone attack and had to rush to a hospital where the doctor could hardly speak English and I was even less fluent in Turkish or whatever his language was.

Cathy turned down a corner of the blanket as I approached the bed. I was disturbed that my penis had shrunk, and was afraid that I would embarrass myself and disappoint her.

"I'm afraid I'm not the best lover in the world," I warned her.

"Let me be the judge of that. I think that most of the men I meet these days are gay."

"I can assure you, that's one thing I'm not."

"But maybe it's just that I don't turn them on."

As she exposed a breast, I said with a smile, "I'm sure that's not the case." .

"You're very sweet, George. You're the sweetest man I ever met."

I wanted to return the compliment and tell her she was the sweetest or most beautiful woman I had ever seen, but neither of these was true, and I was sure she would know I was being insincere.

"Is the pillow okay? It's down. From geese in Sweden.

At least that's what the salesman told me at Pier 1. Gee, I hope you're not allergic."

"It's fine," I said, reluctant to mention that I *was* allergic to down pillows and Alice always bought Dacron or one of the other synthetics. They were also machine washable.

At home, Alice and I had our sexual routine with its impromptu variations, usually disappointing to one or the other of us and resulting in leg spasms and backaches. I didn't know what Cathy was expecting, or what turned her on. If it was something out of Kama Sutra, a copy of which my friend Mac Adelstein had once bought for a quarter at a Good Will store when we were kids, I'm afraid she was out of luck.

"Just hold my hand awhile," she said dreamily.

I took her hand, half-hoping that this would be enough for her, and that she would eventually fall asleep like a kiddy with its favorite toy. But aware of her naked nearness, the other half of me wanted her, wanted her desperately, and I turned over on my side and put one arm about her waist and the other around her buttocks and pressed with all my might while I kissed her. She pressed back just as hard, caressing one part after another of my body.

Till consummation, I was afraid that Frederick would suddenly phone to make up with her and that she would wrap herself in the sheet like a respectable lady and request me to leave.

Afterward, I was nervous while she smoked in bed, and I suffered a leg spasm when I reached over to the night table to get her an ash tray. She told me that a town in Rhode Island was named after an ancestor of hers who had come over on the Mayflower. Another ancestor had taught both Greek and Latin at Dartmouth. His translations were in both the Library of Congress in Washington and the House of Commons Library in London. And his translations of Horace were favorites of both Disraeli and Gladstone, who had disagreed about everything else except the supremacy of the British Empire and the virtue and wisdom of Queen Victoria.

All too soon for me, she wanted an encore, and to do it while she sat on my lap on a chair and I called her Katie. I had an idea it might be a father-complex thing like in so many plays and books these days, but I was reluctant to ask. Later, I got dressed and she accompanied me to the door.

"Don't forget your portfolio," she said.

"No. I certainly won't."

She ran a hand over the canvas. "Do you have occasion to use the thing inside very often?"

"Only now and again. It's mostly for impression management, as they say."

"I never served you your coffee. You must think me a terrible hostess."

"I'll never think that. There were other refreshments."

"I hope you had a pleasant stay."

"It was most pleasant. Thanks for inviting me."

We both looked at the floor for a while. She put a hand on the doorknob.

"Now that you know the address...."

I wondered whether she really wanted me to ever come again. I had a hunch that it was like when couples meet at resorts and exchange addresses at the end of their week together, all the time knowing that their new friendship was, like a ticket to a play, good for only a single performance and not transferable to another time and place.

"Thank you," I said anyhow. "I'd like to come again."

"Please write to me first."

"Of course."

I didn't expect her to give me her phone number, and she didn't.

"Some of my old commercials still pop up occasionally, especially the one for White Velvet bathroom tissue. I have three lines that I say to a man at the counter. 'You're my last hope, Mr. Ross. My husband and kids are so cranky these days. Can you recommend a new bathroom tissue?'"

"I'll look out for it," I promised.

A FTER THE STUFFY and perfumed bedroom, the cold air and snow felt good and refreshing. At least for the first block. Aware of my wet shoes and socks, and hoping that I didn't catch a cold if not something worse, I walked up Lexington Avenue without heading anywhere in particular. Now that the fun was over, I knew that I had done wrong and was angry at myself. Alice had stuck by me even though I had turned out to be a failure in life. Only that morning she had assured me that I was not a failure, that I was selling myself short, that I had suffered a temporary setback but would get a new and better job.

"Anyhow, it isn't as if we were down to our last dollar. I still have my job, thank God, and a little savings."

"No offense to Women's Lib, but I hate not being a breadwinner anymore."

"It's only temporary. And you supported me for many years."

"But that was while the kids were little and you had to stay home."

"Maybe you'll get something today. You're wearing your good suit, I see."

"That's because I'm thinking of applying for secretary general of the U.N."

"Don't sell yourself short. You might get the job."

"I'll phone you right away if I do."

"Phone me whatever, please."

"Don't look so worried, Alice. If you're thinking that I might commit suicide...."

"I'm not thinking that at all, and don't *you* ever. I love you and will love you whatever happens. Call me about one o'clock unless you get the U.N. job and are on your way to Bosnia or wherever. Nowadays, when you turn on the radio and hear immediately about a bombing, it could have been in a hundred different countries. Or in one or more of our own fifty states."

It was now close to two. I came to a phone at the end of the block.

"Hollywood Knits," Alice said.

"It's just me. I'm calling from my office at the U.N., where I'm the new secretary general."

"Good. I knew this morning that all you needed was a little push."

"A little push into the grave maybe."

"What happened—an unpleasant interview?"

"Something of the sort."

"I'm sorry. You sound so depressed. I wish I was with you. I hear traffic. Where are you really?"

I squinted through the snow at a street sign on a lamppost. "Lexington and Sixty-eighth."

"What are you doing all the way up there?"

"I had a lead to something over on Third Avenue, but it didn't pan out."

"Something will come along sooner or later. Don't walk around in the snow too much. Remember your various aches and conditions."

"How can I forget them?"

"Have you had lunch yet?"

"Earlier I had a cup of coffee."

"That's no lunch. Go into a restaurant and treat

yourself to something nice. Is Lexington Avenue where they have that Jewish dairy place with the low-fat vegetable cutlets and that are very reasonable?"

"I don't know."

"Why don't you call it a day for job-hunting and go over to the Frick Collection? You're only a few blocks away."

"I don't feel it would be right to be looking at pictures while you're slaving away."

"I'm not slaving away. Mr. Davis is absent today. No kidding, I'd really like you to go over to the Frick. It'll give you a spiritual lift."

"I don't see how looking at Rembrandt's face is going to help me."

"Then look at the Renoirs. But not at his nudes."

"Okay, maybe I'll go there. Will meat loaf be okay tonight?"

"Fine, but don't forget to move around the egg while you're mixing it, and not too much oregano. Julia Childs is down on oregano these days."

"Maybe she recently had a pizza at that new joint we tried in Sheepshead Bay."

"I can't imagine her ordering a pizza in Sheepshead Bay or anywhere else except maybe on the Via Tornabuoni in Florence, where she always orders the rare herbs and spices for her casseroles with a hundred ingredients and a thousand grams of fat. I'm looking forward to watching the rerun of *The Winds of War* after dinner. Except for maybe Nick Nolte, they don't have actors like Robert Mitchum anymore. In tonight's installment he's supposed to meet Winston Churchill. Or is it President Roosevelt?"

Speaking of world leaders, I suddenly remembered my appointment with Big Nick.

"Damn. I'm going to have to miss tonight's installment. I have to visit someone pursuant to a job."

"Who?"

"Bernie Rhineland. A guy I used to know at work. He's now into renting movies and watching them at home, which is going to replace going to the theater."

"After dinner is a peculiar time to meet someone about a job."

"That's the only time he can make it."

"If you have to go, well, that's it."

"Yes, I do have to go. I really have to go."

"Meanwhile, I see Mr. Miller coming, and I think that I'd better go too."

"Who's he? Another boss?"

"This place is crawling with bosses. Every time a guy marries one of his ugly daughters, Mr. Davis takes him into the firm so he won't get away. I love you."

"I love you too, Alice."

"Give my regards to the Fragonards."

On the next block I asked a doorman shoveling snow whether he knew of a Jewish dairy restaurant in the immediate neighborhood. "Not really," he said, and then pointed diagonally across the street. "There's this other foreign restaurant. They say the food is good and the prices aren't bad."

"Thanks. I may try it."

"But on the other hand, I saw an ambulance pull up there yesterday and then someone was carried out on a stretcher."

While we were on the subject of food, the doorman, Tommy Murphy from County Tipperary, where he wished he was at this moment, told me that for a Christmas gift, one of his tenants, a U.N. official from Hungary, supposedly a civilized country, had given him only a can of stuffed cabbage hardly enough for two portions.

"Maybe next year you'll have an Arab tenant and he'll give you an oil well."

"Them Arabs don't observe Christmas."

"Then maybe for Mohammed's birthday. You gotta have hope in this world."

"So I've been hearing since I was born."

I had a bran muffin and a cup of coffee in a luncheonette and then crossed to the north side of Seventieth Street and started up the block toward the Frick near the corner of Fifth Avenue. Outside of the Frick was where I had met Alice on one of our very first dates. She was working in the neighborhood as a weekend temp in an antique shop. By then, I was already a few years at the *Globe* and still hoping for a break. I saw her coming down the block and I hurried toward her and kissed her, very lightly, since we were in public.

"I'm sorry if I kept you waiting," she said. "Been waiting long?"

Though I would have waited forever for her, I thought it corny to say that. Once again I wondered what she saw in me. We had met on the *Thomas Jefferson,* a Hudson River Dayliner. I was with some guys from my neighborhood in Brooklyn and she was with some girls from hers, the Mott Haven section of the Bronx. We spotted them while the boat was passing Grant's Tomb on its way to Bear Mountain, but we didn't finalize our strategy for approaching them until a few miles upstream at about Fort Tryon Park. My interest was the girl with brown hair in a white blouse and pale blue slacks, who turned out to be Alice. Al Vittachi was attracted to the blonde in red Bermuda shorts. Paul Dimitrio, luckily, liked the third girl, Rita. Al, who later became an assemblyman and then a consigliore for the Mafia in Jersey, thought that he should do the talking, and being on the shy side I did not argue with him.

Al: "Excuse me, girls, but my friends and I are interested in knowing the name of that tall structure over there on the hill."

One of the girls: "It's called the Cloisters, I believe."

Al: "That's very interesting. Do you mean nuns and monks reside there?"

Alice: "It's a museum. It's a museum of medieval art. It's part of the Metropolitan Museum on Fifth Avenue."

Al: "I must visit there someday in the not too distant future. By the way, I'd like to introduce myself and a

couple of my pals. I can personally vouch for their character and good conduct."

Alice: "You can? That's certainly a load off my mind."

Because she had spoken first to Al, I was afraid that
Alice would be attracted to him, but he had yet to become
one of *New York* magazine's best-dressed men and by the
time we passed Yonkers we were already strolling by
ourselves on the deck.

As I walked along Seventieth Street in the snow, I
saw Alice as she had looked on the boat, with the wind in
her hair, and her nose freckles bright in the sun. I remembered that there had been polka dots on her blouse, and
that it was sleeveless, and that her slacks were really pedal
pushers, and that she was wearing tennis shoes. That had
been the happiest day of my life, and I wished it could
have lasted forever.

Today, on the other hand, was one of the saddest
days. For the first time I had been unfaithful to Alice, and
this evening, unless something happened, I would almost
certainly give my commitment to Big Nick and become a
member of his crime family. Maybe I would be better off
doing what Paul Dimitrio did about five years after the day
of the boat ride. He had failed as a violinist and dreaded
being a shipping clerk in the Garment District for the rest
of his life. One day on his way home from work, he jumped
in front of an F train at the Twenty-third Street station.

"Why?" his mother asked me at the funeral and every
time I met her afterward until she died a few years later.

"Why did my son want to be dead instead of alive? He had so much to live for."

Today I could have given her an answer.

A few yards ahead of me on the snowy and windy street, a tall man in a gray hat and gray tweed overcoat emerged from a high-rise apartment building, the sort that was inhabited by celebrities, rich foreigners and expensive call girls. I recognized him at once, and my heart began to hammer and my stomach to churn. My legs turned to rubber, and I had to lean over and grab a railing for support. It was none other than Mr. Warren, my former boss at the *Globe*. I had had many bosses there, but he had been the big boss.

He stood in place on the sidewalk for a while, as if he were undecided which way to turn. I sidestepped so that he wouldn't see me, because I had no great desire to say hello to him. I imagined our conversation.

"Hi, Mr. Warren."

"Well, if it isn't George Mancuso!" Probably he would extend a hearty hand, because smiles and handshakes never cost anything. "What are you doing up in this neck of the woods, fella?" No doubt he thought that I had less right than he to be in this ritzy neighborhood where no less an important personage than the *Globe*'s publisher lived in a town house inherited from a grandfather who in turn had inherited dozens of slums in Albany and Rochester. "What've you been doing with yourself since you left the *Globe*?"

I would lie and say I had a good job.

"Glad to hear it, fella. Hope things work out more satisfactorily for you than they did at the *Globe*. I still think that you made a hasty decision. You were the best mail clerk we ever had and we're all sorry you saw fit to leave, but things downtown seem to be working quite smoothly. Stop in and say hello when you're in the neighborhood."

"I will."

"Keep punching. My regards to the wife."

I would not send my regards to *his* wife, because early last year they had divorced after about thirty-five years....

He glared up at the sky as if willing the snow to stop. His executive influence did not extend up to heaven, and finally he raised his coat collar and turned in the direction, luckily, of Madison Avenue, which meant that our paths wouldn't cross. I waited till he had gained ground, and I then resumed walking though still shaky and light-headed like when I'm in a movie theater and people in the immediate area light up their joints of marijuana.

After a few yards I came to his footsteps, which were larger than mine, and I remembered how he had thrown his foot across his desk that first day. I wondered whom he had been visiting in the high-rise. I thought of the expensive call girls I frequently read about in the *Globe* and other tabloids. According to the grapevine, publishers had a gentleman's agreement to never report the vices of fellow publishers and selected executives and staff. I knew also that a lot of psychotherapists had their offices there. I wondered, though it was unlikely, whether his treatment of me at the *Globe* had finally given him a guilt complex and he was spending a hundred dollars for fifty minutes three times a week to find a cure. If so, I prayed that he would keep spending his money until the shrink took him for his last penny and left him more neurotic than ever.

Until a few months ago, when I left the *Globe,* Mr. Warren had owned a blue Olds, and I now thought that the one he was approaching near the corner was his, and that he would get in and drive off either back to work, or to his elegant home in Bay Shore, Long Island, or to wherever. But he didn't turn toward it. He walked straight ahead to the corner and waited for the light to change, or for a taxi. I stopped where I was, a few yards behind, not wanting to catch up.

A couple of taxis passed but he didn't raise an arm or give his loud whistle for them. Back at the *Globe,* when he saw me down a corridor and wanted to attract my attention, he would give a whistle that I was sure could be heard up on the eighth floor in the publisher's penthouse.

The light changed and he crossed, and then he proceeded on the same north side of the street. I couldn't help noticing that he didn't walk with his usual brisk stride, and I attributed it to a combination of the snow and his recent exertions with a call girl.

I crossed the street and followed him. That is, I was not actually following him. I just happened to be walking along the same street to the Frick Collection, which

Alice had recommended for my spiritual and emotional well-being, and I wanted to do at least one thing she could approve of that day. Perhaps I would even take in a free lecture if they still offered them. In these days of tight budgets, one couldn't count on anything, not even the sort of popular lecture that mentioned gold finger rings in which the Borgias stored their poison until the right moment to slip it into the wine goblet of a cardinal who opposed their candidate for the papacy. I imagined meeting Alice at the door as she returned home, chilled by the walk from the subway. I would be holding our cat, Rocky, in my arms, for otherwise he would run out toward the Kutowski's apartment, where I suspect he loved the two kids more than he did me.

"Hello, honey. How were things at the office today?" (What a wonderful unisexual greeting. Years ago, when our kids were young, it was *she* who asked *me* that question.) "I couldn't wait for you to get home so that I can tell you about the wonderful lecture on Renoir. I'm glad you told me to go. I never knew before that Renoir was influenced so much by Fragonard."

An unpleasant thought occurred to me as I walked along the street. What if Warren were visiting the Frick too? I certainly didn't want to run into him in one of the galleries. Having to speak with him and revive the past would ruin my visit. I wondered if he had ever stopped to think what he had done to my life, to my life and Alice's. I could have been—no, I didn't want to think about the past, about what might have been. Some weeks ago, during a conversation with a friend who was in A.A., I was feeling a little sorry for myself, and I said, "When I think back over all my wasted years at the *Globe*...."

"Don't permit yourself to think like that," Ed Burko said.

"It's easier said than done. When I think back, I feel like killing someone."

That someone was Jack Warren, of course.

I thought of the gun in my portfolio. Though I was out of practice, I had once been a good shot. Walking only a few feet ahead, Warren was a perfect target, and I couldn't have missed his broad back or big ass if I had tried.

In my mind's eye I saw myself taking out my gun and shooting him. It would have been the perfect crime. The snow would have muffled my shot, and anyhow there was no one else on the street. But it wouldn't have been a real revenge in the classic Sicilian style, because he would die without knowing that I, George Mancuso, had killed him.

He came to the entrance of the Frick, and continued walking. A few moments later I too came to the entrance. I paused and looked up past the several steps to the door. I lowered my portfolio from under my armpit and felt first my bag of two paperbacks and then my gun. I turned back to Warren and saw him almost at the corner of Fifth Avenue, in front of him the traffic and the bare, swaying trees of Central Park. The pictures at the Frick could wait another day, but not the death of Jack Warren, and I resumed walking.

I walked slowly, staying close to the fence of the Frick, where, inside, a chandelier lit up the Fragonard Room. I knew from my history class in high school that the French royalty for whom Fragonard had painted were guillotined during the revolution. It seemed a just fate for them. What else should they have expected for oppressing the common people for so many centuries?

The light changed, and Warren crossed Fifth Avenue and began to walk south, downtown. The light was still green and I followed him across.

The wind from the park stung my face and I wished I were wearing my terrific hooded parka from the Alexander's department store in the World Trade Center. Warren walked slowly and I had no trouble keeping up with him, unlike on that first day at the *Globe*. After telling me the room number of the mail room, he had decided, since he had business in that part of the building, to introduce me personally to Al Vann, the mail room head.

"Okay, let's go, George," he said, making a little swipe at his nose.

In the outer office he told his secretary to hold the fort until he returned in about fifteen minutes. He strode briskly along corridors lined with offices with brightly varnished doors. I recognized the names on some of them. Marcus Goldman, the gossip columnist who disliked Liz Taylor and Kim Novak for some reason but did like to mention what he considered their heavy thighs. Phyllis Norton, the consumer columnist whose family owned a chain of hotels, including two in Las Vegas, but wrote as if she would have to apply for federal food stamps if the price of potatoes and eggs ever rose by only a penny.

"They're all very important people, as I'm sure I don't have to tell you," Warren said. "If they don't get their mail on the minute, it can spell disaster. Maybe even cost them a Pulitzer Prize."

"Yes, sir," I said, almost panting with the effort of keeping up with him. Years later I would learn that a *Globe* writer could never win a Pulitzer, because a powerful member of the committee at Columbia University had once been passed over for chief editor after working twenty-two years at the paper. The job was given instead to a San Francisco editor who was a young nephew of Mrs. Drew's dental surgeon. The surgeon had restructured her jaw and teeth after an accident at a golf course in California.

Warren had paused to shake hands with a man with a clipboard who came out of a door.

"Good job today, Mel. I'll bet they'll read it and weep in Albany."

"That was the general idea. Screw the bastards, I say."

On our way again, Warren said to me rather

confidentially, "That was Melvin Pierce, our top editorial writer. He too started at the bottom here, not as a mail clerk but as a copyboy. You can be a copyboy too in a few months."

I nodded.

"And from there you can work your way up to a reporter or whatever your heart desires. Other men have made it and I see no reason why you can't too."

I will *make it,* I said to myself.

I saw myself as a reporter sitting at a desk and rapidly typing a story. I resolved to buy a portable typewriter and increase my speed, which had fallen off since my classes in high school.

Far down the corridor and after many turnings we came to a door with the words MAIL ROOM painted in the center, and Mr. Warren pushed open the door. The room was about the size of my aunt and uncle's living room. On one side, a fat, bald fellow of about thirty-five was feeding envelopes into a noisy machine. The envelopes passed along a belt and fell into a slot on the other end. At the other side of the room, two fellows of about twenty were emptying sacks of mail upon a long wooden table in front of a row of coops such as I had seen in my local post office.

"I'm bringing you a new recruit," Warren said to the fat fellow at the machine. He was one of the fattest people I had ever seen. He had a double chin, and rolls of flesh hung over his belt. He was very well dressed in a white shirt and dark tie, sharply creased pants and dazzling black shoes.

"So what else is new?" he said. He switched off his machine and stared at me like I was something in a toilet bowl. "He doesn't look any improvement over the last two stiffs you sent me."

Mr. Warren put an arm around my shoulders and laughed. "Even the great Joe DiMaggio never hit a home run every time at bat. But seriously, Al, I think George here will work out quite well for you. He's very ambitious to learn the operation and succeed at the *Globe*."

Al Vann rolled his eyes to the ceiling. "Where have I heard that one before?"

Mr. Warren then introduced me to him. I put out my hand, but Al ignored it, and spoke past me to the two fellows at the table of mail.

"What are you two jerks staring at? There's no show going on. We're already late with this delivery."

One of them said, "It wasn't our fault the mail was late."

Al growled something in his throat, and said to Mr. Warren as he folded his arms across his chest, "Okay, I'll give him a try. You really give me no choice."

"Honestly and frankly, Al, I really expect great things from George. I feel it in my bones that he's going to work out for you."

As Warren looked into my eyes, I tried to look worthy of his confidence. I was glad to have him on my side. Having hardly known my father because he died so early, I was deeply moved to know that I was being sort of protected by another grownup man.

"I'll now leave you fellows to get better acquainted," Mr. Warren said, starting to the door. "*Hasta luego,* as the Cisco Kid would say. Don't forget, George, I'm rooting for you."

Al waited until Mr. Warren was gone, and then heaved a deep sigh and said, "Where are the mail boys of yesteryear? Can anyone answer me that?"

"Can I hang up my jacket somewhere?" I asked.

Reluctantly, and with a scowl, Al pointed to a metal wardrobe across the room.

"Bring in a hanger tomorrow," he called after me.

An index card had been attached with masking tape to one of the wardrobe doors. It said: CLEANLINESS IS NEXT TO GODLINESS. THIS MEANS YOU! I supposed that the suit jacket and topcoat on varnished wooden hangers belonged to Al, and that the zipper jackets on wire hangers belonged to the other fellows. The suit jacket and topcoat hung far apart from the other garments, as if there were danger of contamination. I took the hint and hung up my own jacket with the zippered jackets. Attached to the inside of the door was a mirror, and under it a second index card said: THE MAN WITH THE SMILE IS THE MAN WORTHWHILE.

I turned and saw Al standing next to me. My smile did not suggest to him that I was a man worthwhile.

"Have you ever worked in a mail room before?"

"No." I felt like I was confessing to a crime.

"Have you ever worked anywhere before? Maybe you're one of those society playboys."

I told him politely of the jobs I had had since leaving school. Already I was looking forward to being transferred to the city room. To prove my capability and dedication, I would work hard and be the best mail clerk the *Globe* had ever had, just as later I would be the best copyboy and reporter and columnist....

A bus was coming down Fifth Avenue. Mr. Warren suddenly quickened his steps to the curb and took his place in line behind a few other people. Pulling down my hat as far as I could and still not look like a mobster in an old film starring George Raft or Edward G. Robinson, I hurried after him to the line, but stood a little apart and with my head turned to Central Park, as if I were entranced by the scenery there. Actually, as they shook and swayed, the trees reminded me of the Martha Graham dance company that Alice liked to watch on Channel Thirteen. My intention was to wait on the curb until Warren had deposited his fare and was walking up the aisle.

"Are you coming?" the bus driver growled.

Stalling, I said in a disguised voice, "Are you going downtown?"

He grunted, and I mounted the steps and slipped in my token. "Just wanted to make sure," I said. "I'm a stranger."

"You don't say."

A young man of about twenty with a wispy blond beard sat in the first seat. He touched my arm and said cheerfully, "We're all strangers here. And heaven is our destination."

"I certainly hope so. That's the best news I've heard in quite a while."

"Take my word for it." Smiling, he unzipped the black portfolio on his lap. "Or, rather, take the word of a greater authority than I." He removed a black Bible from his portfolio and held it up to me.

I nodded that I knew what it was.

He rose and motioned me to take his seat. "Please, my friend."

"I appreciate your thoughtfulness, but I'm really not that ancient."

"I know that, sir, but I respect not only your superior years but the spirit of God within you."

"Thanks, in that case."

"No problem."

From the seat, I had a good view of Warren sitting across the aisle near the center door. He was touching his chin, and seemed deep in thought.

The young man thrust a hand at me. "Mark Hobby is the name, and salvation is my game."

"Nice to meet you. I'm Frank Miller." Naturally, I was not about to give my real name to a stranger who might be a maniac like in *Psycho*, the Alfred Hitchcock movie. For a few days after seeing it, Alice liked me to be near the bathroom when she took her morning shower.

Mark said, "And it's nice to meet *you,* Frank. Do you mind if I call you Frank instead of Mr. Miller? In the Bible, everyone is called by just a first name, and it makes everything seem so much more intimate."

"I never thought about that."

"There are many things people never think about."

"This may sound silly, but since the patriarchs are Hebrews, wouldn't their full names have been something like Abraham Cohen or Isaac Levy?"

"That's a good one. Mind if I repeat it Sunday at my tabernacle in Bushwick?"

"Be my guest."

"Which reminds me that I promised to bring along a tambourine. It's for a wedding. He's a Reform Jew and she's a Native American, a Mohawk, the tribe that are not afraid of great heights and work on skyscrapers, including the World Trade Center downtown. Please don't ask me how the happy but unusual couple wound up with us."

"Believe me, I won't."

"It's a beautiful day, isn't it?" Mark pointed to the window against which the snow was blowing. "Some people would say it's a nasty day, but seen through the eyes of faith, love and hope, every day is beautiful and radiant."

I nodded that he was entitled to his point of view.

Warren looked thinner than I remembered him. Now that he was divorced, he no longer had his wife's good cooking. I recalled the time I brought a special delivery letter to his office and on his desk happened to be a Corning casserole dish. He explained the dish's presence to me: "The publisher told me recently that he'd eaten lasagna at La Roma uptown and it was pretty good. Today I brought in a batch of the little woman's special recipe so that he could taste what great lasagna is really like."

We were passing Temple Emanu-El, whose Friday night service on WQXR a former neighbor, Hank Rabinowitz, used to listen to. Alice and I were very pleased when Hank invited us to his son Irving's bar mitzvah, not in Temple Emanu-El on Fifth Avenue but in a much smaller synagogue on Avenue R in Brooklyn. Alice and I shopped around a long time before finding a genuine Waterman's fountain pen, which we understood was the traditional gift. About ten years later Irving was killed trying to protect an old woman who was being mugged on Orchard Street in Manhattan, where he worked as a bookkeeper for a ladies underwear company. Hank told me that the fountain pen was among the personal effects he picked up at the morgue the next day. It was Irving's lucky pen, and he didn't usually carry it around, but he was working up some special tax forms for his boss and wanted to make a good impression.

I couldn't see it, but behind me was the Arsenal Building, on the other side of which, near the pool of seals, I had once lost a balloon at the zoo. My mother had just handed it to me, and I was adjusting the string on my fingers, and suddenly it was rising into the air and beyond my reach.

Still on the subject of today's snowstorm, Mark was saying as he tapped on his Bible, "As Ecclesiastes tells us, 'For there is a time for every purpose and for every work.'"

I couldn't have agreed more with Ecclesiastes and with Mark. There was a time for killing Warren, and it was today. I wished I knew where he was going. It didn't seem as if he was going to the *Globe*, or at least going there directly. I took a firmer grip on my portfolio.

In front of me was the General Motors Building where I had met Gertie the Con and her accomplice, and behind me was the Plaza Hotel where I had met Mr. Anthony. By now, I considered myself as definitely embarked upon my second and more successful career as one of Big Nick's zappers, and I supposed I would be a regular customer of Mr. Anthony whenever he came to town.

"No," I would tell him. "I don't like any of these .32 jobs. Nor these Italian ones either, no disrespect to the old country. I think I'll stick with a good old Smith & Wesson .38. I used one on my very first hit and everything went like a charm."

Mark said, "I see that you carry a portfolio."

"I find it very useful for odds and ends."

"Are you carrying a Bible today?"

"Not really. But I've got other inspirational literature."

"Why not stick with the true and tried for thousands of years?"

"You may be right."

"I know I'm right. And Leo Tolstoy is my witness. In addition to his great novel *War and Peace,* he wrote a story called 'How Much Land Does a Man Need?' and I agree with James Joyce that it is the most profound work of literature ever written."

"In that case, I'll certainly look for it in the library. Especially since it's a story and not a long novel like *War and Peace.* My wife is a big fan of Henry Fonda but she thought that he was miscast in the movie version. She had no complaints about Audrey Hepburn, however."

Mark reached deep into his portfolio, moved his hand around, and finally brought out the sort of small black New Testament that an old gentleman, rather a fanatic, used to distribute free of charge outside Trinity Church when I used to make ultra-confidential deliveries to the publisher's stockbroker down the block from the New York Stock Exchange. According to rumor, the Bible man was trying to atone for his long and greedy career in stocks and bonds.

"I would dearly like you to have this Bible and read it every day."

"Thanks, but I know we have one at home. Maybe even two or three."

"But this one is small and portable."

"Don't you need it yourself?"

He smiled as he pointed to his larger Bible.

"Thank you," I said.

"For these trying times, I particularly recommend Matthew, chapter ten."

"Right. Chapter ten. I'll certainly look at it when I get a chance."

I wanted to tell Mark that Warren, sitting across and down the aisle, probably needed his New Testament more than I did, since he had little time to cleanse his soul before his final journey. Warren had put on his eyeglasses and was studying a sheet of paper about the size of a memorandum from Mr. Drew, the *Globe's* publisher. The idea now occurred to me that back at the high-rise he had been arranging for an apartment for Mr. Drew's latest mistress. As all-around general factotum and trouble-shooter for the *Globe,* Warren was often called in to help with the romantic problems of the VIPs. There was the time when I was making my last mail pickup of the day in the executive suite and I suddenly heard Judy Leigh, the charming and sophisticated assistant personnel manager, screaming and cursing like a barroom drunk from inside Mr. Drew's office. Pretty soon Mr. Warren came running up the corridor, and he knocked on Drew's door and entered. Later, in no great hurry, came Bill Daniels, one of the security guards who was hired after the window of Mr. Drew's limousine had been smashed during contract negotiations with several of the unions.

"Better you shouldn't be here," Bill said.

"What's going on?"

Bill hesitated, then couldn't resist telling me a spicy

story, especially since the security guards were now also negotiating for higher pay.

"Drew the Screw is having a little trouble with his latest piece of nookie. The way I hear it, when he first hired the broad, he promised to make her personnel manager when Leonard Yates retired, but instead he brought in a guy with minimum experience but who belonged to his fraternity at Yale. Now Drew wants his daily dose of pussy, but Judy is saying 'no, no, daddy.' Warren's gone in to pour oil on troubled waters. I have to stand by in case of mayhem. Can't wait to retire and hire one of the reporters to ghost-write my memoirs. My spies in the city room have informed me that Drew has a few illegitimate kids tucked away somewhere, and that may be enough to justify the title I have in mind, which is *From Here to Paternity*."

I didn't take Bill's advice and leave, but watched from a corner. As it is said of prisoners that they compulsively inspect every inch of their cell, so I had come to take an interest in every aspect of my own cell, *The New York Globe*. The commotion stopped after a while, and Warren emerged, patting Judy's hand and nodding his head in complete and heartfelt sympathy with her situation. Though she didn't deserve my advice, for she had recently docked me a day's pay when I stayed home with Alice after a miscarriage, I wanted to yell out to her that Warren was shafting her just as he had been shafting me for years.

"Goodbye, Frank," Mark said as the bus stopped in front of the public library on Forty-second Street. "I have to do some research here for a term paper."

"I hope you get an A," I said.

"It really makes no difference. The world is full of sin, and I'm sure Armageddon will be upon us by the time I get my master's degree in computer science. Since you look kind of depressed, Frank, I'd like you to consider a thought from Second Corinthians."

"Shoot. I'm all ears."

"'We walk by faith, not by sight.'"

"Thanks. I'll certainly keep it in mind."

Mark was already at the door when he turned round and addressed the busload of passengers: "Brothers and sisters, there are trying days ahead, but I'm sure that we will overcome them with God's help. Just remember that behind the darkest cloud the sun is still shining. And the same goes for God's mercy. It's always there when you stop to pray and ask Him for it."

"Hallelujah, brother!" said a black woman sitting opposite me. She threw him a kiss. With such vigor and devotion that she would have knocked him over if they were closer.

"God love you all, and have a safe ride and nice day. You too," he said to the bus driver.

The driver squinted at Mark as if he was a lunatic who should be locked up, and the sooner the better.

"And I hope that Mayor Koch comes up with that raise for your union."

The driver managed a smile. "See you in church, fella."

Forty-second Street was one of the busiest streets in town, and I expected Warren to get off there to pursue either business or pleasure. But he remained seated, slowly rubbing his lowered head as if he had an ache. He would have a real headache when he saw me and my gun.

I turned the pages of my new Bible, and read, "And I myself also am persuaded of you, my brethren, that ye also are full of goodness, filled with all knowledge, able also to admonish one another."

I was certainly going to admonish Warren.

"Jesus therefore answered and said unto them, Murmur not among yourselves."

I was through murmuring about my rights the way I used to at the *Globe*. When I shot Warren, I would be speaking out loud and clear.

It had been snowing as hard today as on my first full day at the *Globe*. The Globe Building was at the corner of Chambers Street and West Broadway, but Al Vann had put me on the early shift, which meant that I had to go first to the Church Street post office for a pickup of the mail. Since there would be two or three bags of mail, I would have to take a taxi to the *Globe*. Working with me would be Jimmy Doyle, who was also on the early shift.

I had been told to be at the post office at six-thir-ty. When I awoke at four o'clock, I was afraid that my alarm clock wouldn't go off later, and so I dressed and studied a book I had taken out of the library the evening before: *Reportorial Writing*, by Stanley Fishman, a Pulitzer Prize-winning reporter with the *Washington Post*.

Too excited to eat more than toast and tea, I left home at five. My footsteps were the first in the snow all the way up Avenue U to McDonald Avenue and the F train. From the F train I would change to the A at Jay Street in downtown Brooklyn, and from there it would be only a few stations to my destination in downtown Manhattan. I was wearing the Timex wristwatch that my aunt and uncle had given me upon my graduation from high school.

As luck would have it on my first day at work, a work train was picking up garbage on the A line, and at Jay Street, when I explained my situation to a friendly pas-senger, he advised me to stay on the F till East Broadway and then walk west till Park Row. East Broadway was a decent street with a lot of Chinese stores and restaurants, but Park Row was full of bums lounging or sleeping in doorways. Now and then one would call out to me for a cigarette or a handout. Since I was a Christian and supposedly created like them in God's image, my heart went out to them despite their ferocious appearance, but I didn't have any cigarettes and had only three dollars to last me for the day, and anyway I was afraid to go near them. My fears seemed justified, for many of the men I ignored would shake their fists after me and call me such names as "motherfucker" and "Jew bastard."

At last, after a few blocks along Park Row, I reached the Municipal Building, topped by a statue that I knew from my civics class represented Municipal Virtue, or Civic Pride, or something noble like that.

From there it was a hop, skip and a jump across City Hall Park and down Barclay Street to the Church Street post office. Outside St. Peter's Church on the corner, a large carton of unwrapped rolls fell off the back of a bakery truck. The driver stopped the truck and retrieved them though, true to their name, they had rolled down the street and into the gutter and were now wet and dirty. I recalled what I was once told by a neighbor who was a waiter at a popular restaurant in Times Square: "You'd be surprised at some of the disgusting leftovers that are recycled into our famous meatballs and meat loaf and Salisbury steak. What people don't know will never hurt them."

All along my way from home, I had been hoping that I would meet a friend who would ask where I was going, so that I could answer with justifiable pride: "To my job at the *Globe*."

"The newspaper?"

"Yes, the newspaper."

"Wow! You're with the *Globe*! What do you do there?"

"Right now I'm in the mail room, but in a few months I'll be in the city room."

St. Paul's Church on Broadway, where George Washington had worshipped, was tolling six o'clock as I entered the post office. I waited at the bulk mail window while all five employees ate doughnuts and drank coffee and discussed last night's boxing match. At last one of them broke his heart and condescended to notice me, and I presented the card authorizing me to receive the *Globe*'s mail.

"Another one!" he yelled.

He opened a door and pointed to my two sacks of mail. "All yours. Hope you can get a cab today."

I sat down on the steps in the lobby to wait for Jimmy Doyle. I arose to make way for a man mopping the steps. I sat down again. Six-thirty came but not Jimmy Doyle. By a quarter to seven I became frightened that the *Globe* would not be able to publish that day without the mail, and I started to drag my two sacks across the lobby to the street.

"Hey! What the hell are you doin'?" the floor mopper screamed at the top of his lungs. "Those sacks happen to be U.S. federal government property. And so is this marble floor."

"So...?"

"So, you dumb jerk, you gotta have respect for the government and you can't drag them. You gotta carry them unless you want J. Edgar Hoover and his FBI after you."

I waited another few minutes for Jimmy Doyle, and

then lifted the filthy sacks to my shoulder and carried them out to the street.

A taxi arrived finally, and it pulled over to the curb. I opened the rear door and threw in a mail sack.

"Not on the seat! Not on the seat! Where you going, kid?"

"The *Globe* on Chambers and West Broadway."

"What did they tell you to spend?"

"Sixty cents."

"The cheap fucks. Do you know how much a private mail service would cost them?"

"No, I don't."

"Out! Get that crap out of my cab."

"I'll give you an extra quarter out of my own money."

"I wouldn't take even an extra dollar. I don't wanna have nothin' to do with a crappy paper that hates the working class and supports Wall Street and the Republicans. They don't even have a good sports section anymore."

"If you really supported the working class, you'd give me a ride."

"Out, Mr. Wiseguy! I'm in a hurry."

No other taxis came along, and, though I'd be damaging government property, I had to drag the mail bags several blocks to the *Globe*. If arrested, I could claim in my defense that I had never signed a petition or joined an organization that opposed the United States and its policies either at home or abroad. I regretted, however, that I had never joined two of our patriotic organizations—the Boy

Scouts of America or our local Little League team, the Gravesend Gophers.

At the *Globe* I had to find a maintenance man to open the door of the mail room for me, because Jimmy Doyle had the key. Jimmy arrived at seven-thirty, bearing an English muffin and a container of coffee.

"Sorry I didn't think of getting something for you too. I see you got here okay. I happen to have been a little detained. My grandmother is very sick. Look, you don't have to tell Al about this. Screw him, I say. We mail clerks have to look out for each other."

Al stormed in at nine-fifteen, cursing the subway system, the snow, the sanitation workers who were legally responsible for clearing the snow. He was furious that we weren't further advanced in sorting and distributing the mail.

"Mr. Moore will be phoning any minute. And Miss Goodwin. You know what sons of bitches they are." He jabbed a finger at Doyle's chest. "You keep bellyaching about a raise. But you don't want to work for it."

Doyle protested his innocence with a thump to his chest. "It ain't my fault, Al."

"Whose fault is it then? Is it this other creep's?" Al asked, turning to me.

"Well, it's his first day, and it takes a little time to show him the ropes."

Al said to me, "How come you forgot to tell Warren yesterday that you're Max the Molasses Man?"

"I'm doing my best, Al."

"Your best doesn't seem to be good enough, does it?"

After this pep talk to the troops, Al straightened his tie in front of his wardrobe mirror and went down to the luncheonette to have breakfast on company time. He didn't return till ten-thirty, when he removed a toothbrush from a plastic case and left for another forty-five minutes.

During my lunch hour I ran into Mr. Warren outside the luncheonette in the lobby.

"How's it going, George?"

"Fine."

"Glad to hear it." He thumped my shoulder.

I hesitated, then said, "But Al can get a little rough."

He jerked back and looked surprised by my remark. He shook his head. "Al takes a little getting used to, like caviar and old brandy. But once you know him, I'm sure you'll respect him the way the rest of us do. Anyhow, you won't be in the mail room forever. I have my eye on you, fella."

Since the luncheonette was crowded, Mr. Warren asked me to order a few things for him and bring them up to his office on a tray. I welcomed the opportunity to be of service to my benefactor.

At Thirty-second Street, the bus turned off Fifth Avenue and headed west toward Penn Station. Warren and I were the only passengers left, and I held the *Times* over my face. I imagined that after a free day in the city he was returning home to Bay Shore. I knew his address because I had often put his personal mail through the Pitney-Bowes postage meter that was supposed to be used only for business mail. At Christmas, he, like other VIPs, would come into the mail room with boxes of their personal greeting cards. And of their wives' and husbands'. I was surprised when it was done even by Dr. Sally Cooper, who wrote a weekly column on ethics and good behavior, once advising a Catholic reader to confess to her priest that she was tempted to report him to the police when she saw him hosing down his black Buick during a severe drought emergency when people were advised to shower less frequently. Warren had said, "Just run these few letters through like a good lad. I'll straighten out the bill with Ben Oliver in cashier."

A few years later, riding down the elevator with Ben when he was half-stewed after a Christmas party, I asked him whether Warren ever came in to straighten out his postage bills. He said with a wink, "Are you kidding? Why should he be different from the other VIPs? And if I were you, I wouldn't ask questions like that. If you were in their shoes, you'd probably do the same thing. In fact, you would have to. The other VIPs would consider you a dumb schmuck if you didn't. It's like the politicians in Washington who ignore the traffic lights that average Americans like us have to observe. And please don't get me started with the call girls in Washington."

Approaching Seventh Avenue, the bus driver called out wearily, "Last stop."

I continued holding my newspaper till Warren was walking out through the rear door, and then I rose and followed him. I slipped my Bible into my pocket, thinking it a desecration to put in into the portfolio with the gun. Following Warren across Seventh Avenue toward Penn Station, where the Long Island Railroad Station was located on a lower level, I noticed how crowded the street was, and thought that here would be an ideal place to kill him and then lose myself in the crowd.

Yes, I would be a man of decision. I would kill him now and be done with it. My legs weren't as good as they used to be, but they would carry me two or three blocks to safety. So what if I suffered a few spasms later on? I had almost a full prescription of Soma tablets at home. Unzipping my portfolio, I followed Warren onto the sidewalk, meanwhile looking to my right and left for cops. A well-dressed young man, a junior-executive type out of *Gentlemen's Quarterly,* stepped between us.

"Are you selling, man?" he said with the glittering smile of the rich seeking something from their social inferiors.

"Selling what?"

He pointed to my portfolio. "Come on, man. Don't put me on. The stuff. Are you selling the stuff, man?"

I realized that he was referring to marijuana or cocaine.

"Sorry, man," I said. "What made you think I—?"

"Fuck! I have a presentation in fifteen minutes." He rushed off toward another man with a portfolio.

By this time Warren was descending the escalator. Other commuters were waiting their turn on the escalator, and I took the staircase, watching Warren massage his stomach as though relieving an ache or cramp.

Reaching the bottom, he stepped aside from the flow of traffic for a minute and continued rubbing his stomach. Finally he lowered his arm and resumed walking slowly toward the interior. I wondered how old he was, and estimated that he was in his early sixties. When I came to work at the *Globe,* he was still being referred to as the Boy Wonder. Later the title was taken over by a younger Boy Wonder who had once worked for Rupert Murdoch in London. This journalistic genius was going to raise the *Globe*'s circulation to a million within the year. But when it never even approached that figure, he was fired abruptly and an item in the business notes column said that he had resigned in order to pursue other interests.

Coming to a pharmacy, Warren walked past the door, but then he turned around and went inside. Afraid that the store had a second entrance by which he might leave, I followed him in and walked along the aisle after him until he stopped at a shelf and removed a box. Seeing no other entrance, I left the store and stationed myself across the corridor.

He came out opening a package, and slipped one

of its contents into his mouth. He looked at his watch, but apparently his train wasn't pulling out immediately, because he walked no faster.

When he paused in front of a window display in a photography shop, I stayed far away so that he wouldn't see my reflection. He stood there a long time, rubbing his brow, and as he and then I walked on, I turned my head to see what had interested him, and saw that the display featured Disney World.

Over a Fourth of July, Warren and his wife and two children, Johnny and Claudia, had visited not Disney World but Montauk, and one day he sent me out to a photography store on Chambers Street to pick up his pictures of the outing. He seemed in a particularly good mood when I returned to his office, and I seized the opportunity to bring up something that had been preying on my mind for weeks.

"I hope I've been doing a good job in the mail room."

He reached for the envelope of pictures and his change. "You've been doing a great job, George. Keep up the good work, pal." He removed the pictures and began to examine them, now smiling, now frowning. He put on his eyeglasses for a better view. Looking up from the pictures, he seemed surprised to see me still in his office.

"What's douchin', fella?"

I had been dreading this moment for weeks, but I couldn't put it off any longer. Finally I took a deep breath and said:

"You promised me, Mr. Warren."

He took off his eyeglasses and frowned. The creases in his brow made him look older and harder, like Sam McReady, the head cashier, when he threatened to report to Mr. Drew those employees who asked for their weekly paychecks even a few minutes before the official time.

"What did I promise?" Warren planted his elbow on his desk. A pinkie picked at his nose.

I was so nervous that I could hardly speak, and wished I hadn't begun.

"Go on," he prompted, and stared at his watch as if I were keeping him from an appointment with Mr. Drew.

"You said that after three months I would be transferred to the city room."

He looked stunned by my statement. He leaned back in his chair and began to swing his arm. He rubbed his brow with a couple of fingers as if he were massaging his memory. Finally he said, "Is that really your impression of our conversation?"

"Yes, sir."

He shook his head and smiled, inclined to be generous and forgive the impetuosity of youth. "I think you've gotten it a little wrong, though it's a natural-enough mistake. When I said three months, *if I even mentioned that particular time period,* I used it merely as a figure of speech."

I did not really understand what he meant, and I tried not to look too dumb.

He laced his fingers together and rested his chin on

them. "Three months...or six months...or whatever period. What I had in mind was a certain incalculable period of evaluation, if you get what I mean." He leaned forward. "Do you?"

"I think maybe I do, but I'm not sure."

"Let me ask you a question, George. How old are you?"

"I was nineteen the other week."

"Happy birthday. If I'd known, I would have sent you a little remembrance. Sorry."

"It's okay."

"You're nineteen." He closed his eyes as if recalling his own nineteenth year. Then he reopened them with a smile. "You have all the time in the world, and I know a lot of guys who wish they were in your shoes. Don't you think it's better to be nineteen than forty-nine or sixty-nine?"

"I suppose so, but...." He had me confused. I was beginning to think that I had been unreasonable to bring up the subject at this time.

He picked up his photographs. "Rest assured, George, that I have you on my mind and haven't forgotten about you. When the time comes, you'll certainly have your opportunity. You have to know how to walk before you can run. Meanwhile, you're making very decent wages for a mere high-school graduate and you're also getting valuable experience for which other young men would give their eyeteeth." He riffled through the papers on his desk. "Every day I get these impressive resumés from college graduates. Some of them attended Fordham and Columbia, no less."

Leaving his office in another minute, I apologized in case I had offended him by my ingratitude and haste. He gestured that all was forgiven.

And now, many years later, we had reached his day of reckoning, and the place was the concourse of the Long Island Rail Road. Warren selected a paperback from a wall rack in a newsstand, paid for it, and sat down in the waiting room. Still keeping an eye on him, I walked over to the rack of timetables and picked out the one for Bay Shore. The train wasn't leaving for another eighteen minutes. I joined the line at the ticket window. On an adjoining line I saw a former acquaintance from my neighborhood, and I turned my head so that he wouldn't notice me and try to engage me in a lengthy conversation.

I returned to the waiting room, where I felt very professional about my tailing of Warren, as if I were already an experienced member of Big Nick's family. At the ticket window I had coughed and held a tissue over my face so that the clerk couldn't see enough of me for a description to a police sketch-artist, if it ever came to that.

Warren was ignoring the conversational advances of the slender young man now sitting beside him who might have been a hustler, and finally he looked at his watch, leaped up and rushed away. He stopped at a lunch stand for what looked like a glass of milk, which he drank slowly and thoughtfully.

Not being a commuter, I could not understand most of the announcements on the loudspeaker, but Warren evidently did, for he gulped down the rest of his milk and then hurried off to a staircase. Following him down the stairs, I lost him in the crowd a few times, but I finally spotted him walking down the platform and entering a car.

When I reached the car, I saw to my surprise that it was not the smoking car. He had always been a heavy smoker, going through at least two packs a day.

"Everyone needs to have at least one vice," he used to say, implying that he himself had no others. "The worst vice," he remarked to me on one occasion, "is ignorance."

I wondered at the time if this was a reference to the fact that I had not yet enrolled in college. I did try to correct that shortcoming after beginning to work at the *Globe* in late January. I did a lot of studying and reading on my own, as I still do to this very day, and in early September I went up to Hunter College to enroll in their night school.

After sitting around for two hours I was finally called into an adviser's office. He was a short man, bald, and in a bad mood for some reason, or for no reason at all, because it was just his nature. Immediately, his phone rang and he rushed off without so much as an "excuse me," not that I had really expected one, being a mere would-be student. During his long absence of almost a half hour, in order to make constructive use of so much idle time, I began to read the copy of the *Times* on his desk. Returning, he scowled at me and growled, "Are you in the habit of just helping yourself to other people's property?"

"No, of course not." I folded the newspaper and returned it to his desk. "I'm very sorry."

My folding was not to his satisfaction, and with a glare more homicidal than all of Charles Bronson's in *Death Wish 1, 2* and *3* put together, he picked up the newspaper and folded it to his satisfaction, which was no improvement over mine. Then he snapped out a hand for the transcript of my high-school record. After skimming through it in record time, he said, "This is not a particularly distinguished record, is it?"

"I guess I'm not exactly Albert Einstein."

"You can say that again." He sighed. "If I may ask, Mancuso, what did you do in high school except goof off?"

"I don't think I goofed off."

Shaking his head, he read off some of my marks. "I hardly think you were trying very hard to make a success of your career in high school. Your parents should have gotten after you a little harder."

I didn't like to talk about my personal situation, but I had to under the circumstances. "I didn't have any parents to help me."

He stared at me as if I had committed an incredible act of negligence. He said finally, "Are they both dead?"

"My father is. My mother was sick all the time I was in high school. I guess I just couldn't concentrate on my studies."

"Four years is a long time to be sick."

"She was mentally sick. And she never recovered."

"Oh. But regardless...."

"When I came home from school she'd be crying or doing peculiar things like tearing up the curtains. It was hard for me to concentrate on homework."

"You should have studied in the public library. There are libraries all over town."

"I guess I was too depressed."

"Other students have persevered under similar conditions. Think no further than Abraham Lincoln, the Great Emancipator of our country."

After additional talk he informed me that my average was not high enough for admission to Hunter, though I could enter as a non-matriculating student, paying for my courses in the hope that my grades would be good enough to enable me to switch to credit status eventually. His sniff said that he didn't hold out much hope of that. He suggested that if I really wanted to get a degree, my only realistic hope was that I apply for admission to a small private college. He mentioned one in Buffalo, which was far away at the other end of New York.

"Do you know how much they charge?"

"Whatever they charge, it'll be worth it in the long run. A college education is beyond monetary consideration. Although, frankly speaking, after looking at your record, I wonder if you are really college material. It's nothing to be ashamed of. Some of our finest citizens have not gone on to college and yet lead useful, valuable lives and are a credit to their country and to themselves."

But his expression said that if they *had* gone on to college, their lives would be even more useful and valuable. He thrust my transcript at me and looked over my shoulder at the door.

"Sorry I can't be more helpful. You might consider going back to high school at night and trying to raise your average."

I left his office in a great depression, envying the fellows and girls in the corridor who were walking around with catalogues of the different courses and with all sorts of registration forms. I tried not to feel resentful toward God that He had not seen fit to provide me with a home atmosphere conducive to sound studying habits.

I entered the train and watched Warren walk down the aisle and finally sit down. I followed and sat down about five seats behind him on the opposite side of the aisle. There, I took out my *Times*, to have it ready to put in front of my face in case he had to return my way in order to visit the bathroom. The car filled up and a tall, heavy man with a thick mustache and beard stopped and smiled down at me.

"Mind if I sit here?" he said, gesturing toward the aisle seat.

"Not at all."

A bell rang and the train was moving. My plan was to zap Warren along the road from the station to his house.

I had been out there twice. Once, while he was home with the flu, Mr. Brownell, the comptroller, had sent me out with some important papers that needed his immediate attention and signature. On another occasion, while he was on vacation, I had brought out some books from the *Globe* library that his daughter needed at once for a term paper. On my first visit, it was Mrs. Warren and not the live-in housekeeper who opened the door of the large white building, the kind featured in TV commercials where a happy family is seen in front of the garage, and then the husband drives up in the new Ford or Chevy that will assure them a lifetime of joy, especially in the bedroom. His wife had looked uncomfortable in my presence, as if she wasn't sure how to behave with a mere mail clerk and not a member of her own class.

"Is that George?" Warren called out from inside.

I was led into the den where he was sitting in a blue silk robe on a leather sofa, watching a baseball game on TV. Within arm's reach on a cocktail table was a glass of red wine and a bowl of potato chips. He didn't look all that ill to me, and I wondered how Al Vann would have reacted if he had seen me looking like that on a sick day.

"As you can see for yourself, this flu has really drained my vitality," he said. "I feel like a zombie in a horror movie. I hope my wife and kids don't catch it from me."

"Sorry to hear that, Mr. Warren."

"Have to drink juices and other liquids till it's coming out of my ears. If that isn't enough, the Yanks are four runs behind. I can't imagine what's gotten into them."

I groaned in sympathy. And, like a true Yankee fan, including Sister Harriet, a nun at my church, I tried to look like my world would come to an end if the Yankees lost this particular game.

He offered me a glass of orange juice for the road. His wife brought it in from the kitchen. The color was less bright than any of the standard brands in Brooklyn supermarkets, and the taste was flat. I was sure it had been diluted, which didn't surprise me. On the TV, Mickey Mantle came to bat with two men on base and hit a homer.

"Wow!" he shouted, and leaped up in his red velvet slippers and slapped my back with quite a lot of strength for an invalid.

Since he was suddenly in this good mood, I decided to bring up the subject that had been on my mind.

"I've been in the mail room almost a year and a half now."

His smile said I could be there forever if I wanted to. "And I think you've been doing a bang-up job. Keep up the good work, lad. I hope Al hasn't been on your tail again. If he has any gripes, just tell him to see me. You worry too much about him. His bark is really worse than his bite. I happen to know from various sources that he thinks highly of you and your work."

"Oh...?"

"Rest assured about it."

"I heard recently that there's going to be a copyboy job open in the near future. Milton Zimmerman is leaving. He's gotten a sports job with a paper in Denver."

"Denver isn't that great a town," he said, and spoke about it a few minutes. He mentioned a Denver restaurant where the famous barbeque and onion rings had once upset his stomach and ruined the rest of his drive out to California.

I nodded my sympathy for his stomach and ruined vacation and said, "I'm interested in having a crack at that job. I hope you'll put in a good word for me with Don Spector. I understand that he's in charge of hiring copyboys now."

Warren put a hand to his mouth and chewed a fingernail. Then he knit his brows and stared hard at me. "Honestly, George, do you think you're ready for the city room yet?"

"I think so. I have an idea of the duties that would be required of me. I've been studying journalism."

"Oh? At which college?"

"I've been studying on my own."

"In other words, you're not enrolled in either a public or a private college."

"Not presently."

"You told me that you were going to enroll last year," he said, looking a little sad, as if I had disappointed him.

"Things didn't turn out."

He nodded that he understood the situation. "I guess your high school average wasn't up to par."

"I hadn't fulfilled some of the science and language requirements."

"I see."

"So if you'd please mention me to Don Spector at some time in the near future, I'd be very grateful."

"Of course. It would be my pleasure, though of course I can't guarantee that anything will definitely come to pass. As you probably know by now, Don Spector is a pretty funny guy."

"I could speak to him myself, but I thought that, coming from you...."

"Let me see what I can do. Are you really firm about your decision to move on from the mail room?"

"Yes. I am."

"I happen to know that everyone admires and respects you and your work."

"I'm really pleased to hear it."

"Even Miss Costigan in the penthouse, and you know what a crab she is."

"I've never thought she was such a crab, really."

"Somehow, I can't imagine the mail room without you."

"Al Vann will still be there, and that's what's really important."

"Yes, but an army needs troops as well as a general."

As he led me to the door, he assured me that he would try his darnedest for me....

Aboard the train to Bay Shore, the conductor came up the aisle and punched my ticket. The bearded man beside me had come on without a ticket, and he paid cash. "How far out is Amityville?" he asked the conductor.

"Forty-one minutes."

"Thanks, my friend." The conductor having passed along, my seatmate turned to me and said with a laugh, "I hope the place I'm visiting doesn't turn out to be another Amityville horror."

I hadn't read the former best-seller, but knew it was about a house inhabited by demons from the past.

He pointed to the inscription, *Sunshine Tours,* on my portfolio. "May I inquire if you're in the travel business?"

"No. I'm merely a traveler."

"We are all of us travelers, whether or not we're on vacation."

"That's true, I guess."

"But this afternoon I'm a literal traveler, out to Amityville, whose name will turn out to be symbolic. Or so I hope."

"It may have been settled by Quakers."

"Sounds quite possible." He put out his hand. "Stuart Kurtz. No relation, thank God, to Mistuh Kurtz." As I shook my head, he added with a grin, "People sometimes ask me that as a joke. The guy is a mysterious African trader in *The Heart of Darkness* by Joseph Conrad. Sooner or later everyone is assigned to reading it in school. That and *Jude the Obscure* by Thomas Hardy. Kurtz's dying words are, 'The horror! The horror!'"

"Referring to what?"

"Maybe to some of his dealings in ivory and maybe slaves. Maybe to just life in general and what may be awaiting him in the hereafter. I guess that only Joseph Conrad knew for sure. And, of course, teachers of English lit. They always know better than the authors themselves, or so says Kurt Vonnegut, whom I once met at an Irish bar on Third Avenue."

I decided against giving him my real name, in case the police tried to trace me after the murder. "I'm Phil Lanza."

"Glad to meet you. Any relation to the late, great Mario Lanza?"

"No, though I certainly liked his singing and movies."

"His youthful death was a terrible tragedy. As my Yiddishe mama used to say at our hacienda on Tremont Avenue in the Bronx, 'The old must, the young may.'"

"My own mother used to say something similar in Italian."

"I guess death comes to all races, religions and creeds. And, of course, sexual orientations. It's an equal opportunity employer, as the saying goes."

"I'm glad there's equality in *something*," I said.

"You sound a little down on our American system."

"Not really."

"Maybe the time has come to change some of your mutual funds. It can often do more good than changing therapists. Or so I've heard."

"I'll certainly think about it," I said, and looked off toward Warren. I couldn't see him, but I supposed he was reading his paperback, maybe a thriller like he used to get from Cynthia Spring, the *Globe*'s literary editor, in return for a favor like procuring illegal Cuban cigars for an author she'd been dying to interview. The author was never a government official of either party, because they could get all the cigars they wanted despite the boycott against Fidel Castro. I wondered what Warren would be doing or thinking if he knew that this was his last hour on earth. Would he be praying?

On the Sunday after asking him to speak to Don Spector about me, I went to church with Uncle Lou and Aunt Josephine and I prayed that I would be acceptable in the eyes of the lords who guided the destiny of the city room. I didn't know any of them personally, but from what I saw of them as I passed through with my mail, they were a tough, snarling, angry bunch of men, often with a cigarette in the corner of their mouth, often jumping up and bawling out a reporter across the desks. I was rather glad I didn't have to approach Don Spector myself, though I would if it became necessary.

All the next week I waited to hear the good news of my transfer from Mr. Warren. Whenever I left a batch of mail in his outer office with Estelle Cutler, his current secretary, I expected her to look up from her typewriter and say that her boss would like me to step inside. One midweek afternoon I passed him walking in the corridor but he looked preoccupied and I thought it best not to approach him just then.

On Friday, while making one of my rounds, I asked Estelle if Mr. Warren was free to see me for a moment. She knocked on his door, entered his office and returned.

"He says he's been very busy and hasn't gotten around yet to your matter, but he very definitely hasn't forgotten about you."

I prayed in church again the following Sunday. On Thursday I saw Mr. Warren coming toward me along the corridor on the penthouse floor. We came together by a window that looked out on the Hudson River and New Jersey.

"Hi, George," he said without slowing down.

"Do you have a minute, Mr. Warren?"

He looked at the folder in his hand and then at his watch. "Okay, just a minute." He tapped the folder. "It's that time of the month, you know."

"Have you had a chance to speak to Don Spector about me?"

He snapped a lighter to the cigarette in his mouth. He then looked as if the cigarette was disagreeing with him. "I did," he said.

"And...?"

Looking away from me, he placed his foot on the windowsill and gazed out over the river.

"I'm afraid it's no dice, my friend."

I found it impossible to believe. I felt weak suddenly, and was afraid my legs would collapse.

"Believe me, I tried my darnedest. I used all the eloquence at my command." His nod added that Abe Lincoln and Daniel Webster would have been envious of him.

"What did he say?"

Mr. Warren closed his eyes in an attempt to recall Don Spector's exact words. "He said, in short, that he wanted someone with more journalistic background."

"Did you tell him I've been here a year and a half?"

"I told him. Believe me I did. I must say for Don that he was a gentleman and listened to every word of my pitch. But in the end, he seemed to feel that the mail room was not exactly the background he wanted at the present moment for the present job opening. Anyhow, I gathered that he was already pretty settled in his mind about hiring some other young person."

He removed his foot from the windowsill. He patted my back.

"That's it, I'm afraid. I'm really and truly sorry I don't have better news for you at this moment in time. Perhaps I will upon a future occasion. Keep slugging, champ. Don't look so dejected. There'll be other opportunities coming along." He tapped the newspapers under my arm, and made a gentle smile. "You'd better get along with those. The publisher just saw the new Media Records and he's in one of his famous moods. I guess we're all going to have to put our shoulder to the wheel and push a little harder."

His smile said he was confident that I would push as hard as the next guy. He pounded my shoulder and set off toward the elevator. I stared out of the window a moment, and then followed him. He turned his head but continued walking.

"Anything else, George?"

I blinked to keep the tears from my eyes. "When you hired me, you promised me that...."

"Let's speak a little more softly, like two gentleman."

"I'm sorry if I raised my voice."

He nodded that he forgave me. Before we could resume our conversation, Alex Caulfield, the national advertising manager, stepped out of the men's room a few feet ahead. He adjusted his tie and bent over to polish his shoes with a tissue. About fifteen years later he was to die of a heart attack while sitting in a booth in that same bathroom. He had always been hard on his salesmen, and the joke went around that he had died in an appropriate place.

"Hi, Alex. You look terrific. I like your suit."

"Hi, Jack."

"Sorry about those figures."

"You can't win them all."

"Tell that to the publisher."

"You're not kidding, fella."

Caulfield passed out of hearing.

"A great newspaperman," Warren said. "He started as a newsboy in Staten Island, which is as low as you can get. And now he's one of the VIPs. I'd advise you to take him for a role model."

"When I started here, you assured me that I would be in the city room in three months."

"Assured. Is that really the word I used?"

"Well, maybe it isn't the exact word, but it's certainly the drift of what you said."

"I think you're putting words into my mouth. Prod your memory a little harder, and see if you won't agree with me that I said, rather, that I would try my darnedest, or some such expression. Thanks for upgrading me, George, but I'm not really an important personage on these premises, and I'm in no position to assure anything for anyone. I don't think I'm influential enough to assure my own kids of a job here if they were old enough to work already."

"I don't think I can take Al and his abuse much longer."

"Is that what's really bugging you?" He put a hand on my shoulder. "First chance I get, I'll tell him to ease up on you a bit." He laughed. "Maybe I'll have more pull with Al than with Don. You'd better get along with your papers."

I made a snap decision. "I don't think I'm still happy working in the mail room."

"Hell! I'm not particularly happy in my job either. Do you know of anybody who is?"

"I think I would like to resign."

"That's up to you, of course, George. You're a free man. America isn't Russia, thank the Lord. But I'd advise you very strongly, as I would my own kid brother, to sleep on your decision. The *Globe* is going to expand big within the next few years, and golden opportunities will be sprouting up all over the place. Being a valued and trusted employee, you'll be in the best possible position to step in." He slapped a fist against his palm. "Do you know something, George? I think so highly of you both as an employee and an individual that I'd like to do something for you, not in the future but right now. What's your salary these days?"

Despite Mr. Warren's painting of a bright picture for me in the future, and his promise to seek a raise for me, I still felt depressed, and passing the window on my way to the executive suite, I lingered there a while, and imagined myself jumping out to my death.

Mr. Warren was true to his word upon this occasion. About two weeks later, when I met him in the lobby, he whispered to me that my increase would appear on my next check but I was not to mention it to any of the other mail clerks. The increase turned out to be for $4.95, and I wondered for a long time why it hadn't been for an even five dollars. I was sure Mr. Warren would have told me that the extra nickel would have caused all sorts of tax and accounting complications that I could not even begin to imagine.

About fifteen years later, on the night of a free lecture by Paul Duke, the famous print and TV newsman, I saw Don Spector sitting at the bar at the Newspaper Guild headquarters on Forty-fourth Street. Fired from the *Globe* after taking a sock at Bill Mankers, the managing editor, he was on a shit list and had been unable to get an editor's job in the metropolitan area and was now freelancing articles for *New York* and other magazines. I was afraid to approach and question him cold sober, but with two drinks under my belt, I was finally bold enough to sit down beside Spector and ask why he had refused to give me a chance in the city room. He had shaved off his beard because he was now also an adjunct professor of journalism at Hunter College and, according to gossip at the *Globe,* he had been told that this new look made him resemble Richard Burton somewhat, which would attract enough female students to guarantee his job for the semester. Pulling at his now hairless chin, he told me that he could not recall that Jack Warren had ever made a pitch to him for one of his kids in the mail room.

"I swear to God that if I'd known, I would have been happy to give you a whack. A degree in journalism is almost a must now, unless of course you're a big shot's lover, friend or relative, but in those days it wasn't all that essential. I know for a fact that Bill Mankers, for one, never spent a day in college, and I always had strong doubts that the son of a bitch even finished kindergarten."

I was awake all that night of my meeting with Don Spector, wondering if he had only played buddy-buddy with me. It was unbearable to live with the knowledge that Warren had lied to me. I imagined myself killing him in a dozen different ways....

Sitting beside me on the train, Stuart Kurtz opened his briefcase and removed a pint bottle of Hiram Walker's blackberry brandy.

"Long rides always disagree with me, and I find that this stuff helps settle my stomach. Can I interest you in a snort?"

I would have liked a drink for my nerves, but was afraid of leaving fingerprints on the bottle he extended to me.

"No, thank you."

"Cheers, in that case."

To make things harder for the police who would be trying to track me down, I said to him, "I'm traveling to Lindenhurst to visit relatives."

"From a train, these Long Island towns look all the same to me. I've just gotten back to New York after more than twenty years in L.A., and I wish now I'd stayed there. Do you remember Patty White?"

"The name is vaguely familiar."

"Once upon a time she used to sing with the big

bands and even had a program on the radio. If memory serves, her sponsor was Lady Diane cosmetics."

"Of course I remember her. She was almost as popular as Dinah Shore and Patti Page for a while."

"You've got it." Kurtz returned the brandy to his briefcase and removed a pile of music paper. "The dame is thinking of a comeback, and her manager has asked me to come up with some special material for her. That's where I'm off to now. I'm meeting her at her manager's place. He's Harry Abelstein."

I shook my head that the name didn't mean anything to me.

"He used to be associated with, I believe, Liberace."

The name still didn't ring a bell.

"By the way," he said, "I hear that, despite all the airs and graces that were mostly part of his shtick, Liberace was one of the nicer guys in show biz."

I remembered what Cathy had told me, and said, "I hear that, on the other hand, Irving Berlin wasn't such a friendly guy."

"With over a billion dollars in the bank, Irving could certainly afford to be distant and aloof. But the rest of us have to scratch each other's backs until our fingers bleed. I don't blame Irving, however. He was a Jewish kid from the Lower East Side, his folks were immigrants from Russia, and on his way up the ladder he, like everyone else, was treated like shit unless they had the right contacts or didn't mind to be auditioned on a couch. Now he can enjoy all the perks of being on top of the heap." He looked at his fingers and bit off a hangnail. "Speaking as an old Patty White fan, would you pay money to see her perform again?"

"My wife and I don't go to night clubs, but I would certainly watch her on TV."

"She's still got the pipes, but she's fifty-three."

"I don't think that's so ancient. It's the prime of life, in fact."

"For guys like you and me maybe, but I'm not that sure about a vocalist."

"I say give the girl a chance. In fact, upon further thought, maybe I *would* pay to see her in person."

"I met her at the Carnegie Deli last week. She's a blonde now, and she's still got the boobs, which, I would say, count for about thirty-eight percent in a café gig. I'm sure a scientific poll about boobs has been taken by one of those outfits that politicians hire. Her toosh and legs too are still okay to look at, but she had to join Weight Watchers to keep them that way. She could have only two French fries at the deli, and without pouring on the Heinz ketchup that she loves, because she was born in poverty in Chicago and it's sort of a status symbol to her. She would even put ketchup on her scrambled eggs and oatmeal. Can you just imagine something like that?"

"Go figure," I said, because he was expecting a reaction from me.

Kurtz put on a pair of half-moon glasses and un-clipped an automatic pencil from the breast pocket of his tweed jacket. "I'd like your layman's opinion," he said, tapping the music paper. "How does this grab you for a title of a sophisticated-type of torch song: 'Foggy, Foggy Blue'? It's a spin-off, of course, on 'Foggy, Foggy Dew,' the folk song or whatever it was that Burl Ives used to sing."

In the first years of our marriage Alice and I used to stay in Manhattan after work and take in some of the cheap folk song concerts at Washington Irving High School. We never heard Burl Ives there, but I recall that we heard Pete Seeger and Oscar Brand among others. It was on our ride home from one of these concerts, though they weren't called concerts then but songfests or jamborees, that Alice brought up the subject of having kids. By that time I had had a three-month tryout in the credit department but had failed and was back in the mail room. I was putting in a daily hour of overtime and was also working an overtime day on Saturday. We decided to go ahead and have a baby. Alice had faith that my luck would change, that an opportunity would open up in one of the other departments.

During summer vacation that year I visited the Jew-ish Federation Employment Service and took an aptitude test. The counselor, a Mrs. Fuchs, said that I had a definite aptitude for journalism and saw no reason why I couldn't succeed in that occupation. This made me laugh so much that I wanted to cry. As for the present, the only job she had available was in the shipping department of a famous cosmetics company. Their shipping department was dirty and noisy, and though I passed the interview and was offered the job, I decided to stay with the *Globe* for the time being. There, at least, the physical atmosphere was better and I had seniority in my department.

Always terrible in mathematics, I also flunked a tryout in the circulation cashier's department soon after that. My attempts to get a balance at the end of every day threatened to give me ulcers, which Mr. McReady, the head cashier, already suffered from. One payroll day I made a joke that we should grab the money and take the next plane to South America. He scolded me, saying that theft of company money was nothing to joke about. Many years later, a few months before his retirement, he himself was convicted of embezzlement and sentenced to three years in prison. Joe Keegan, one of the local reporters, told it around the luncheonette that the district attorney had been willing to allow McReady, in view of his age and clean record, to cop a plea that would avoid imprisonment, but Mr. Drew, the publisher, had insisted upon the letter of the law, and he threatened to support a rival candidate for district attorney in the next election, which was only months away.

It was not long after my brief stint with McReady that, after knocking around the country in small opera companies for many years, my neighborhood friend Larry Belmonte switched to popular music, was successful, and seemed likely to become maybe the next Frank Sinatra or Perry Como. When we met at the wedding of a mutual friend where he sang "Because" and had all the women screaming like during an orgasm, he asked me to become his chauffeur-bodyguard when he came back to New York from the West Coast. I said "sure" at once, and bought a used Chevy to brush up on my driving. And, through the good offices of Big Nick, I received an introduction to Rudy Savino, his associate out in the wilds of New Jersey, who taught me dirty fighting and how to use a gun. Whenever I told Alice I was going fishing on Sunday, I used to drive out to the Jersey shore all right, but to practice my fighting and marksmanship at a secluded area owned by the syndicate. On my way home I would buy a variety of fish from men who had actually gone fishing. Alice said that the fresh air was bringing the roses back to my cheeks, and that the fish, though they were a pain to clean, were as good as the offerings at Rossi's Sanitary Fish Store on Avenue U. Though it still bore that name, the store had been owned by a family of Vietnamese for a few years, and whenever Alice or I came in, they were always eating not fish but Chicken McNuggets from the McDonald's next door.

But one night, while relaxing between shows in Las Vegas, Larry Belmonte made out like Flynn with a chorus girl who happened to be a mistress of the silent partner of the hotel where he was performing. Poor Larry's body, minus his beloved penis, was found the next morning in the parking lot behind a supermarket in Castroville, California, which claims to be the artichoke capital of the world. I guess that Castroville was chosen because of its resemblance more or less to *castrato,* a singer who was castrated so that he could hit the high notes in early Italian operas. Impressed by my new skills, Big Nick offered me a job which I was either too law-abiding or too cowardly or too stupid to accept. "Okay, stay in your fucking mail room," he said, "but the job will always be there for you. Unlike some of the scum-bag politicians who are listed on almost every page of the annual voting guide of the League of Women Voters, Big Nick never forgets a pal. Or an enemy, it goes without saying."

Some years later I became assistant head of the mail room, with a ten-dollar raise and the responsibility of running the department in Al Vann's absence, which was frequent, because the union contract provided for a generous amount of sick leave for longtime employees. On the day of my promotion, Mr. Warren assured me that I was next in line for Al's job.

But Al's retirement was far in the future, and he was such a hypochondriac that his constant consumption of pills and yogurt, and herbs and vitamins made it unlikely that he would die an early death, not that I wished it upon him except now and again. I paid a visit to a vocational guidance service, and upon their advice signed up for a ten-month course that would qualify me for work in television production. Upon my completion of the course, I discovered that the field was densely overcrowded here in New York, and my only offer for a job interview came from a local station in Cody, Wyoming. I couldn't follow it up. My mother was by now in Pilgrim State Hospital out on Long Island, and the only thing she had to look forward to in life was my Sunday visits, though she often mistook me for her brother Giorgio, who had died in Naples in 1930 after being kicked by a horse in a carnival. The irony was he had served in the Italian cavalry all through World War I and was never injured. Go figure.

Because of a special mailing to advertisers, I had to work late on April 2, 1975, and entering the apartment I looked at Alice standing in the foyer and knew immediately that something was wrong. My first thought was that something had happened to one or the other of our two children. Alice had just gotten off the phone after a call from a social worker at my mother's hospital. After more than two decades behind their walls and bars, she had just died of a heart attack.

I had long ago given up any hope of her recovery, and I had in recent years thought of her among the dead rather than the living. But after coming home from the funeral, I began to cry without control, and then I saw zigzag lines like colored lightning before my eyes, and my stomach and chest felt as though a skyscraper had fallen on them.

Maybe because the ambulance was operated by Orthodox Jews with skullcaps, I was taken to the emergency room of Maimonides Hospital, where my condition was diagnosed as mostly nerves. After two days of observation and eating a lot of matzos, because it was Passover and I didn't want special treatment because I was Catholic, I was released with a prescription for Valium and the advice from my social worker, Mrs. Oppenheimer, to stay home from work for the rest of the week and take it easy and relax with mystery stories by her favorite author, Agatha Christie. They were never violent and the victims usually deserved to be either poisoned or shot or stabbed, according to the time or place. I was to forget my mother and the past and look forward to the future with my wife and kids. But I found it impossible to forget the past. I thought of how, with money, I could have taken my mother to a private hospital where she might have been cured and been able to spend her last years at home with the family.

I went into a depression that took years to really go away. The simplest task became a great effort. I no longer enjoyed my usual books or music, or going to the movies or watching TV. I became a heavy cigarette smoker, and for the first time a heavy drinker. Often on payday I would stop off at a bar on Coney Island Avenue and stay there drinking and spending money until Alice came for me.

Once I really hit bottom and, because of emotional and physical reasons, was out from work for two weeks though my doctor had recommended three and given me a note to that effect. On the day of my return, Al Vann made a crack that some people believed in coddling themselves.

Over the years he had been absent about ten days to my one. I saw red, and grabbed him by the throat with one hand and punched him with the other. After getting up from the floor, he ran out of the mail room to report me to Mr. Warren. Warren returned with Al and fired me for gross insubordination. I reported my dismissal to my shop steward, who called for an emergency meeting of the grievance committee. Fortunately, Mr. Drew was out of town, and Mr. Reynolds, the general manager, a gay to whose boyfriend I had once donated blood, agreed to the union's proposal that I be reinstated upon condition of good conduct in the future.

To atone for my sin against Al, I worked harder than ever, and in time I seemed to be back on my normal terms with Mr. Warren and Al. I was sorry when Mr. Reynolds died of a stroke during a bargaining session for a new union contract. Because he had been decent to me, I attended his funeral service at Campbell's on Madison Avenue. And I wondered there how many of the well-dressed young men in the chapel had been his lovers. In his eulogy, Mr. Drew said that Bob Reynolds' philosophy of love and truth, and of justice and equal opportunity, would always be a precious heritage to him and to everyone at the *Globe*. However, in the next weekend edition, his monthly column opposed raising the New York State minimum wage by the two whole dollars that the governor had suggested on *Meet the Press*.

At the Red Cross I also contributed a pint of blood

for Mr. Warren when he came down with colitis and had to undergo surgery. He sent me a nice little note of thanks while he was recuperating at home. Returning to work, he never referred to the blood, not that it was such a big deal.

Sitting beside me on the train to Bay Shore, Stuart Kurtz touched my arm and said, "What did the conductor just say was the next stop? Did he say Amityville?"

"It sounded like it. Anyhow, it sounded more like Amityville than Salt Lake City."

"You're a card, Lanza. I think maybe you should be collaborating on this stuff with me. Patty is a pretty demanding broad. I'm not sure that Stevie Sondheim and Neil Simon together would satisfy her."

Warren was rising from his seat up ahead. Coatless, he stepped out into the aisle and walked to the end of the car, obviously paying a visit to the bathroom. When he stopped in front of it and the door wouldn't open, he retraced his steps and then continued walking, heading for the bathroom in the car behind.

"May I look at one of those songs?" I quickly said to Kurtz. "I've always wanted to see what an original song looks like in the process of creation."

"Be my guest. Here's one I have in mind for her closing number. I call it 'Hanging In.'"

I held the music close to my face as if I were nearsighted. As Warren approached, Kurtz removed his briefcase from the aisle though it wouldn't really have blocked him.

"Sorry," Kurtz said to him. "I bet you haven't seen a

briefcase like this in centuries. It was a bar mitzvah gift from my Uncle Herb who was in the leather and luggage racket. He said it would last forever and so far it has. I now consider it my lucky briefcase and plan to bequeath it to my son although he probably wouldn't be caught dead with it and will throw it away at the first opportunity."

Warren said in a smaller voice than usual, which I wouldn't have recognized, "What do kids know about what's important? I hope you continue to use it for a long time to come."

"Thanks for the thought."

Warren having passed on, Kurtz turned to me and pointed his pencil at the sheet in my hand.

"I hope you can read my writing, which makes people ask if I'm also a doctor. 'Hang in, though the skies are gray. Hang in, they're not here to stay. Somewhere, the sun's still there. It still shines, and will banish care.' It needs some polishing, I admit, but you can get the general idea. What do you think?"

"Very nice. Reminds me of Cole Porter."

"Really?"

"I swear."

"It may be a trifle corny, but it's directed to an older audience, sort of a present-day counterpart, if it exists, to the Lawrence Welk and Guy Lombardo crowd of yesteryear. Guy is the only entertainer to whom I ever sent a fan letter. It was something my heart told me to do. My New Year's Eves haven't been the same since he died."

"Mine too. Honestly, I think the song is terrific. I look forward to seeing and hearing Patty singing it at the Waldorf-Astoria or wherever."

"I'll tell Patty you said so."

"Please do."

"I know she'll welcome the encouragement. She's shit-scared about this comeback. She thinks her fans have forgotten her."

I shook my head. "No way."

"The poor broad had that drinking problem a while back. And she bombed pretty disastrously in Vegas some years ago. It was a mistake to have her open the same week as Sammy Davis, Jr., who's a superstar and in a class by himself, appealing to whites and blacks, Jews and goyim. Her manager and PR should have had their heads examined. Ever since then, the poor dame has had the confidence of a jaybird in a hurricane. That's a line by Tennessee Ernie Ford. We once met at a cocktail party in Beverly Hills. Naturally, it was sponsored by Jack Daniel's, which is based in Tennessee."

"Please tell Patty from me, 'Men and women may rise on stepping-stones of their dead selves to higher things.' I recall reading that once in *Reader's Digest.*"

Kurtz slapped my thigh in joy. "I love that! And it gives me an idea for a brand-new number. 'Stepping Stones.' Usually, it happens to me while shaving or while I'm suffering from constipation and just sitting in the john." He began to sing: "Higher, let's go higher. To the sky we'll go. We'll never look below." He slapped my shoulder this time. "Boy, am I ever glad I ran into you. I suddenly have a great inspiration. I'm staying over with Patty and Harry for a couple of days until, hopefully, we have her act shaped up and hammered out. How about giving me a ring there, and then I can introduce you as an old pal of mine who's a true-blue fan, and when she comes on, you can tell her of your loyal devotion over the years and how you're looking forward to seeing her again. I think it'll give her a bigger boost than a dozen visits to her shrink and to meditation and yoga classes were."

"It'll be a pleasure. I'd be happy to help her."

"And you'll be helping me too. I need that advance from Harry to pay my back taxes. On the other hand, careerwise, a few years in a federal prison with minimum security did wonders for some of Dick Nixon's aides. I believe that one of them even became a minister when he got out. Of course it would be much harder for me to become a rabbi, even a Reform rabbi. Gee, I wonder if they'd let me bring my piano into my cell."

"I suppose your lawyer would know about that."

"I'm sure he does, but the s.o.b. would charge me plenty for the answer, even though I once arranged for a cut-rate five-piece band for his nephew's wedding reception at the Chateau L'Amour in the Bronx. He was really pissed off a year later when the former lovebirds got another lawyer to arrange for their divorce because the other guy was a few bucks cheaper."

The conductor appeared in the aisle and announced that we were arriving in Amityville. Kurtz removed a card from his wallet and scribbled down the phone number of Harry the manager. After handing me the card he reached up for his suitcase from the rack. At that moment Warren passed up the aisle on his way back to his seat. I was afraid that Kurtz, an extrovert, would turn to chat with him again and, in the friendly way of show biz, introduce me as his old buddy Phil Lanza. But Kurtz didn't notice him and Warren passed on.

I returned the music and Kurtz stuffed it into his briefcase. He reminded me to give him a ring tonight or tomorrow. He shook my hand as if we were old buddies from Brooklyn or the Bronx or Beverly Hills. With the suitcase in one hand and the briefcase in the other, he walked up the aisle singing.

"Higher, let's go higher. To the sky we'll go. We'll not look below. Let's forget what's done. Think of the—" He hesitated, then turned round and called back to me, "Not to worry, Phil. It'll come to me. Even if I have to plagiarize from Cole Porter."

"I'm sure it will," I replied.

Immediately, as the words came out of my mouth, I realized that I'd made a mistake, that Warren might have recognized my voice.

Quickly, slouching down in my seat, I opened my portfolio and put the *Times* over my face. It was still turned to the want ads, and I remembered the employer

I had called from the bar, and then I remembered Cathy and what we had done in her bedroom. Feeling guilty, I sought solace in the Bible that Mark had given me on the bus, and I turned to Matthew, Chapter 10, as he had suggested. I read: "And when he had called unto him his twelve disciples, he gave them power against unclean spirits, to cast them out, and to heal all manner of sickness and all manner of disease.... And, as ye go, preach, saying, The kingdom of heaven is at hand. Heal the sick, cleanse the lepers, raise the dead, cast out devils: freely ye have received, freely give."

The tiny print was hurting my eyes, and I closed the book. Amid the rattling of the train, I heard a cough up ahead which I recognized as Warren's. It sounded like one of his smoking coughs though he wasn't smoking now. I remembered that he always used to light a cigarette before giving me some news either pleasant or unpleasant. He had lit a cigarette on October 18th, the day he gave me the most unpleasant news ever.

I returned the Bible to my pocket and unzipped my portfolio. I inserted a hand and wrapped my fingers around my Smith and Wesson .38, which my shooting instructor back in Jersey had recommended as the best all-purpose weapon.

One day in mid-September I was sitting with a cup of coffee in the Globe luncheonette when Sam Hanover from the subscription department sat down next to me. He had worked in the mail room years ago, and though he was now in charge of home delivery we were still friendly, at least friendly enough to share a corner table in the luncheonette. First we chatted about Drew's new circulation drive, which included a guess-the-celebrity contest with a first-prize payoff of a trip to Vegas for two. Then he said: "I hear Al is leaving shortly."

"Huh?" I had almost choked on the bagel I was eating.

"He's retiring. He's packing it in after forty years. He's getting his severance pay and buying a condominium in Florida where he'll have a king-sized medicine chest for all of his fuckin' pills."

This was news to me. I had stopped thinking of Al's retirement. I knew he was about sixty-five, but he was getting a decent salary though its exact amount was a deep, dark secret, and he came and went as he pleased, and was absent more often than all of his staff combined. The grapevine had it that early in his career at the *Globe*, Al had somehow, like in a French movie, managed to become the lover of Mr. Drew's sister Cornelia, the family eccentric and ugly duckling, and she had stipulated in her will that, in return for screwing services extraordinary, he be well treated forever after. This was certainly one explanation of his charmed career at the paper, but I had never really believed it, if only because Al had a morbid fear of germs and I could not imagine him kissing and inserting his penis, even with a condom, into Cornelia Drew, even if she did own a lot of stock in the paper and its affiliates.

"I can't believe it," I told Sam.

"Believe. Believe. I got it straight from, well, never mind. I was pledged to secrecy, as they say in the James Bond movies."

"Are his initials J. W.?"

"J. W., or BVD or CBS. It was maybe something like that, but what does it matter?"

"When is Al expected to retire?"

"In a few months. Before the cold weather comes. Al's astrologer told him that another winter in New York would affect his prostate condition." Sam took a bite of his sandwich, which consisted of tuna and melted cheese on an English muffin, and was called tuna delight. It delighted him so much that it was the only sandwich he ever ate there. "I'm sure that you're going to be the new mail room head when Al takes off."

"I sincerely hope and expect so after all these years."

"I'm sure of it. You deserve the job, and you certainly know the work better than anyone else in the world. You're a fixture just like the American flag on the roof. How long have you been there exactly, if you don't mind my asking?"

I was embarrassed to say. Sam had spent only a year in the mail room before being transferred to circulation. Of course, it hadn't hurt that his father was a circulation inspector and used to play poker with Matt Deegan, the circulation manager.

"Almost thirty years," I said at last.

"Wow! That's almost a lifetime. In that time my son Eric the C.P.A. was born, grew up, finished school, married and had a kid of his own. How'd you ever stick it out in that dump upstairs?"

"It's a mystery to me too."

"Well, now at least you'll have this little consolation for your golden years, as they say. Let me be the first to congratulate you, and I hope you're as smart as Al and steal just as many stamps and petty cash and ballpoint pens every week."

I joked that I would steal twice as many though I really intended to remain honest. Superstitious about counting unhatched chickens, I accepted Sam's congratulations with the smallest of nods.

I had intended to return immediately to the mail room after lunch, but I was so excited by Sam's news that I went out for a walk.

I thought of the day I came to the *Globe* for the first time. How the personnel had changed over the years! How the building had changed! How the neighborhood had changed! People had died. Among them Mr. Warren's first secretary. And Ben the elevator starter. And Hal Schaefer, a fellow mail clerk who was killed in an auto crash on the New Jersey Turnpike.

Across the street from the *Globe* for many years was a greeting card store, and its attendant was a blonde as attractive in the same ways as Marilyn Monroe. I had recently seen her on Ocean Parkway, gray-haired and fat, and pushing a baby carriage with a screaming grandchild. About ten blocks south of the Globe Building, shops and tenements and small office buildings had once occupied the site of the World Trade Center. Smoking a pipe, a young man used to stand in the doorway of a haberdashery on Cortlandt Street and urge men to come in and inspect his stylish sweaters and slacks and jackets. He was Sy Syms, and now he appeared in TV commercials telling about the designer clothing he offered to men and women in his stores all over the metropolitan area, and he was also rich enough to give grants to Channel Thirteen.

I didn't know how much Al earned, but it was certainly much more than I did. I thought of the good use to which I could put the additional money. First of all, Alice and I would finally get out of our rut and look for an apartment far away from Avenue U. I would buy her attractive clothes, and we would vacation abroad and for longer than a week. The children were both grown up and living away from home, but when we visited them, we would bring gifts that would dress up their apartments, and we would invite them to dinner and a Broadway show. My son liked clothes, and I would treat him to a new suit, maybe from a Sy Syms store. My daughter loved the ballet. I would treat her to *The Nutcracker* or *Sleeping Beauty* at Lincoln Center.

I tried to imagine how it would feel to be the department head and "free at last" from Al as the Reverend

Martin Luther King, would say. I would be efficient but at the same time considerate of my staff. I would not jump at them when they came in a minute late. I would defend them when Machiko Ryan, the dance and music critic, complained to Mr. Warren that they had set down her mail in the wrong place on her desk. According to ancient principles of Japanese design, the mail should have been placed, very gently, in a designated area in harmony with her karma and nowhere else. At Christmas I would not hog all the gifts of liquor from department heads. I would distribute them fairly.

The conductor was standing in the aisle near the door, and he was announcing, "NextandlaststopBabylon-BabylonchangeherefortheMontauklinedon'tforgetyourbe-longings. HaveanicedayBabylonnext."

I zipped up my portfolio. The train began to slow down. I looked out the window and saw a pond that was mostly covered with ice. The snow was not falling as hard as before. The trees, ground and rooftops were white, or gray rather, for day was ending and the sky was already darkening.

I waited till Warren had left by the front door, and then I left by the rear one. The train to Bay Shore and beyond that to Montauk was waiting across the platform. Warren looked up at the sky before entering it. During my last months at the *Globe* I had several times come into his office with a special delivery or registered letter and seen him looking out of the window up at the sky, and

I once wondered if he had become a bird-watcher since maybe seeing a documentary about John James Audubon on *Nature*, which was Alice's favorite program on Channel Thirteen while mine was *Masterpiece Theater*.

I entered the car by the rear door, and since it was only a single stop to Bay Shore, I remained in the vestibule.

I showed my ticket to the conductor. His punch was like the one we had in the mail room. Early in my employment I found it in the back of a desk drawer when I was looking for something else.

"What do we use this for, Al?"

"We use it to punch holes in kids who ask too many dumb questions when they should be sorting the mail."

I supposed that it would be best to kill Warren along the road from the railroad station to his home. I remembered that the distance was about a half mile. First there was a street of small houses, and then came a stretch with bushes on one side of the street, and on the other a wire fence around a building that had looked from the rear like a library or a small school.

My heart and head throbbed as I neared the great moment. I had come a long way. There was no turning back. Justice and self-respect demanded that I do what I had come to do.

I hoped that the conductor wouldn't remember my face. Years ago I had been told by a fast-sketch artist in Washington Square Park that I was hard to draw because, unlike Mayor Koch or Fred Astaire or Peter Lorre, I had no outstanding features. Her remark had disturbed me at the time, but it was now a comfort.

The train was slowing down. I walked over to the other side of the vestibule and turned my back to a woman lugging a large suitcase and a carton.

"Watch your step getting off, madam," the conductor warned her. "Let me help you with those."

I certainly watched my step at the *Globe* after hearing that Al was retiring. I tried to be even more efficient than usual. The paper had increased its circulation and was now almost up to the *Post*, and one day when I passed Mr. Drew standing by the elevator I handed him a final edition in case he didn't already have one and I said, "Congratulations on that last circulation increase, Mr. Drew."

"Why, thank you, George."

As usual, it gave me a dopey pleasure to know that he knew my name just like he did Governor Carey's and President Reagan's. Both had visited him here when they were running for office and digging for every last vote.

I continued, "I wouldn't be surprised if we were running ahead of the *Post* in a few months."

"That's the general idea."

"I'm sure you'll make it."

"Your warm wishes, George, will certainly inspire us."

Days and weeks passed. At first I wasn't going to do it, but finally I told Alice of Al's retirement.

"Good riddance to that bastard, that beast. When's he leaving?"

I couldn't tell her, because I didn't know myself. Neither Mr. Warren nor Al had spoken to me on the subject. A few times Mr. Warren had come into the mail room and whispered to Al in a corner, occasionally glancing in my direction. Always, on these visits, Al would order me to deliver an envelope or package or send me to the post office.

One day the telephone rang while Al was out of the department on one of his expeditions. Being next in charge, I picked it up.

"Mail room."

"Hi," a young woman said. "Mr. Al Vann?"

Her voice was unfamiliar, and I wondered if she was connected with one of the stockbrokers he was often on the phone with.

"He's out of the room just now. Can I help you?"

"When is he expected back?"

"It's hard to say."

"I'll call again later. Thanks."

"Want to leave your name?"

After a long pause she said, "No. I'll call again."

Al returned about an hour later. He went straight to the wardrobe for his dental floss, toothbrush and toothpaste.

"A woman called but wouldn't leave a name."

Without looking at me or acknowledging my message, he put back his dental stuff and went out the door again.

About two o'clock that afternoon, as I returned to the mail room after distributing the second edition of the *Globe*, Al was sitting at his desk with his back to me. Without turning around he said, "Jack Warren wants to see you right away."

What could Warren want me for but to inform me of my promotion? I hurried to the elevator, for by this time Warren had an office on the penthouse floor.

We were in Bay Shore and the train was stopping. The conductor emerged from the car and took his position near the steps leading down to the platform.

"Bay Shore. Bay Shore. Watch your step, folks."

The passengers included a blind man with a Seeing Eye dog. About a foot and a half of snow had been cleared along the center of the platform. Up ahead I saw Warren walking toward the street.

I climbed down the steps and took the blind man's arm. He was about seventy and wore a black coat and a red knit hat with a patch of Snoopy.

"Thanks. Thanks," he said. "How'm I doing?"

"Great. One more step. Be careful. Looks slippery."

"Ice doesn't bother me at all. Used to be a skater. Ever hear of the Massapequa Marauders?"

"Sorry, I'm new to the Island." I spoke from deep down in my throat in a disguised voice, so that he couldn't identify me later in a vocal equivalent to a lineup.

"You missed some great hockey."

"You can't have everything in this world."

"And that's the truth. Seems to have stopped snowing."

"Just about."

"Nothing like the blizzard of '68," he said with a laugh.

I had been the only one in the mail room to show up for work on the day of the blizzard. When he came in the next day at around noon, Warren, having learned of my devotion to duty, slapped me on the shoulder.

Now Warren had disappeared behind a row of taxicabs.

The blind man bent down and patted his dog. "Sandy is a good soul. I wouldn't take a dozen humans for him. For one thing, dog food is a lot cheaper than Big Macs." He laughed at his joke.

I led him over to the clearing in the platform. "If you walk straight, I think you'll be okay from here on."

"Thanks, my friend. I know this station like the back of my hand. My son's on the police force here. Any time you have trouble with a parking ticket or a meter, just ask for Andy Dressler and tell him you're a friend of his old man's."

I couldn't help asking, "Would it work for more serious crimes?"

He laughed again, and pressed my hand. "Depends on what they are. But you don't sound like a bank robber to me, mister."

"Sure you'll be okay?"

"I'm fine. I'm fine. With Sandy's help I could even climb Mount Everest if I wanted to, and if I had enough of my special garlic pills from Germany."

"What's special about them?" I asked, because Alice was into vitamins and supplements and had an account at GNC.

"Don't get me started, because I could go on for hours."

He squeezed my hand and released it. I hurried after Warren, hearing behind me the blind man talking to Sandy as if he were a person and understood every word. I hoped he got more response than I had ever gotten from any of my cats over the years. Perhaps I should have switched to a dog at some point, but all my life, ever since my father's call to the ASPCA, I had felt morally committed to cats.

I reached the part of the platform leading to the street and turned and saw Warren at the wheel of his Oldsmobile. The motor roared and the wheels strained in an attempt to get a grip on the snow and turn. I prayed that they wouldn't. I had already made my plans to kill him in a certain way and I didn't want to change them. It was unlikely that anyone else would be in his house, and I intended to pursue him there if necessary, but there would be the danger of fingerprints and unforeseen complications.

Suddenly the car was rolling, crunching away from the curb and turning onto the road. I cursed big gas-guzzling cars as I tugged down my hat, turned up my collar and trudged after it.

Nervous tension and the cold weather gave me the urge to urinate. I was afraid to go into the bar and grill I passed, and when I came to an unattended construction site, I walked behind a pile of crates, all from China, and while I did my thing, it occurred to me to that in recent years, whenever Alice and I went shopping for a toy for a kid, we had to look long and hard before we found one that was made in America and not in China or Japan. I wondered how long it would be before American workers would be completely replaced in one way or another.

On the day that Al Vann told me to go up to Mr. Warren's office right away, I had also had the urge to urinate, but I put it off in my eagerness to hear the good news about my promotion.

By this time he had advanced to having *two* attractive women in his outer office, one a secretary and the other a clerk.

"Mr. Warren wants to see me."

"Go right in, George," the secretary, June Neilman, said. "He's expecting you."

Betty Maris, with a curious half-smile, gazed at me from her desk.

Mr. Warren was standing at the window, massaging his back. He turned to me and said, "Thanks for coming up so soon." He pointed to the chair diagonally in front of his desk. "How've you been these days?"

"Fine."

He sat down in his revolving chair and picked up a letter opener that soon found its way to a nostril. I had once read in Dr. Sonja Feidler's Wednesday column that nose-picking was a subconscious desire to masturbate and the cure, as usual, was psychoanalysis.

"And how are things down in the mail room?" Mr. Warren asked.

"Okay. Pretty much the same."

"Good." He tapped slowly on the edge of his desk awhile. "Al Vann has been with the paper a long, long time, as you know."

"I know."

"But all good things must come to an end, including employment at the *Globe*."

I hoped that my nod indicated both reverence and nostalgia.

Warren heaved a sigh. "One of the reasons I called you in is to inform you that Al Vann will be leaving us in the very near future."

"No kidding? This is the first I've heard of it."

"Yes, Al feels that the time has come for retirement."

I was not hypocrite enough to say that I or any of the other mail clerks would miss him. What I did say was, and it was the truth, "The place won't be the same without him."

"You can say that again. I guess that Al has become an institution here at the *Globe,* a monument to service and dedication."

A monument more like Grant's Tomb than the Statue of Liberty, I said to myself.

Warren picked at his upper teeth with a thumb before continuing. "His absence is going to leave a great gap in the mail room."

I felt obliged to go along with his line of bullshit. "There's a gap even when a mail clerk is out on vacation for a week, or out sick for a day."

"That's very true. The mail room is an important department, and it's important to keep it functioning at full, maximum efficiency."

"I certainly go along with that."

"Good, George. I'm glad we agree." He rubbed his hands together and then massaged his thigh. "And now the second reason that I called you in."

I looked eager to hear his second reason though I knew what it was.

"How long have you been with the *Globe*, George?"

"Thirty years, roughly."

"Wow! How time flies." He passed a hand through his hair, which was still abundant though with a lot of so-called distinguished gray at the temples and higher up. "We two go back a long way at the *Globe*."

"I guess we do, Mr. Warren."

"Was Bob McInerney still here when you came?"

"Yes, and for a few years after."

"I ran into him in Vegas last summer. He assures me

he still has no trouble in getting up the old pecker. And he's eighty if a day."

"I guess it's because they have a lot of gorgeous show-girls in Vegas."

"That's very funny. I'll have to tell it around."

I shrugged modestly.

"Your long record of service indicates your dedication to the *Globe*," he said, suddenly more serious.

"I've always tried my best."

"I know you have. And I know also we will continue to have your best when Ms. Merman takes the helm on Monday."

It took me a few seconds to believe I was hearing him right. I felt socked in the stomach and banged on the head at the same time. A force seemed to be flattening me down to the floor. I was finally able to speak: "Who's Ms. Merman?"

Warren leaned back in his chair and folded his hands over his stomach. "Pat Merman is a very capable young woman, and I've been hearing great things about her."

"I've never heard of her. Is she with the *Globe* now?"

"No. But you can be sure she'll make her presence felt when she takes over on Monday." He sat up and leaned over the desk. "Just between you and me, George, don't you agree that the mail room has been needing a shot in the arm in recent years?"

"Is she experienced in mail room work?"

"She comes to us most highly recommended."

I wondered whether this meant, as it so often did, that she was a friend, mistress or relative of a VIP.

"What about me?"

His eyebrows rose in amazement. He made a humming sound in his nose.

"You've told me on numerous occasions...."

He looked at me as if I were an unreasonable kid who had suggested an additional bedtime story. He placed his elbow on the desk and propped up his chin, waiting for me to go on.

"You've always told me that I would be the next mail room head."

He knit his brows in deep concentration, trying hard to remember the past. He slowly shook his head.

"I remember very well," I said.

"I think you're remembering what you *want* to remember."

"I'm not. You made a commitment."

"Com-mit-ment?" He wrinkled his brow as if he had never heard of the word. Or as if a mere mail clerk had no right to use it.

"Whatever word you want to use."

"I gather that you...." With a shake of his head he erased his words and began again. "I can see that you had entertained certain expectations. I'm terribly sorry to disappoint you."

"Is that all you can say?"

"What more is there? To the best of my recollection, as I have already indicated, I never at any time—"

"You did."

"I think we're beginning to talk in circles, George."

"I've spent a lifetime here."

He sat back and sighed. "You're not making it easy for me, fella."

"It's not exactly easy for me either." I squashed my eyes to keep from crying.

"You will still be a valued employee."

"But I won't be as valued as Pat Merman."

"Pat Merman has certain unique qualities."

"What are they?"

He appeared shocked by my question, as if I'd said something in poor taste, like denying that his wife was as beautiful as Ava Gardner in her prime. "I don't think this is the time to discuss them. Take my word for it that she has a lot going for her."

"Who is she related to?"

"What do you mean?"

"Whose girlfriend or relative is she?"

"You know as well as I do that we don't do things that way at the *Globe*."

"Since when?"

He put a clenched hand to his cheek. "Let's not say anything we'll regret later." He lowered the hand to his desk. "Anyhow, the matter is settled. Settled and approved of, I might add, by the very highest authority here. I hope you're not upset because Pat is a woman. If you are, I think it's unfair of you. Women have long enough been denied equal opportunity in industry."

"I would feel the same if it was a man, anyone who came out of left field and—"

"She's not coming out of left field, as you put it. She's highly qualified."

"In what way is she more qualified than I? Does she know the building better? Does she know the postage rates better?"

"I don't want to discuss all that and provoke bitterness. Take my word for it that she's highly qualified and will be an excellent department head. I think that you and the other mail clerks will be very happy working with her. I've had an extremely satisfactory chat with her. She has wonderful plans for the department."

"I have wonderful plans too. Would you like to hear them?"

He looked at his watch. "Why don't you tell them to Pat when you meet her Monday? I'm sure she'll be interested in them."

"Why should she if she's so unique and capable?"

"Please give her a chance. I know that you'll come to respect her as much as I already do."

"I've worked thirty years at the *Globe*, Mr. Warren."

"You've already mentioned that, I believe. As senior

mail clerk, I'm relying on you to cooperate with Pat to the fullest extent during this period of adjustment while she's learning the ropes."

"I thought that she's experienced and already knows the ropes."

He picked up a paperweight and tapped it against his desk. "Are you giving me to understand that you do not intend to cooperate?"

I wanted to tell him to go to hell together with Pat Merman. But I bit my lip and kept silent.

"You haven't responded to me, George."

"I don't think you're really interested in me or anything I have to say. You've never been interested. Have you?"

He rose. "I hate to be blunt, but you're rather forcing my hand. Your responsibility as an employee is to follow the orders of your superiors, and my order to you now is to cooperate with Ms. Merman to your fullest capacity and ability. Follow *her* orders too. I think that can be the only way to run a department and maintain maximum efficiency and harmony, and you would too if you were in my position, which is not a particularly happy one at present."

He came out from behind his desk, and offered a smile and a hand. "I'm willing to overlook your little lapse of a minute ago. Now I would like your word that you'll do what I ask of you."

Within easy reach of my hand was a crystal ashtray

on a little table, and I felt like throwing it at him. I felt like cursing and hitting him.

He continued: "I hope you don't intend dragging out this chat into an all-day affair. I'm sure we both have important work to do. Let me wrap it all up in a nutshell for you. Pat Merman is highly qualified and has already been hired. You are to assist her to your utmost capacity. If you don't, it'll certainly be brought to my attention, and there'll be consequences which I'd rather not discuss at present. That's it."

He walked toward the door, gesturing me to follow him.

"I believe I have some rights under the union contract."

He crossed his arms over his chest. "What rights are those in the present instance?"

"The right to first tryout for any job opening in my department."

"I know the contract pretty well, but I don't remember such a clause. You're confusing the clause that applies to subordinate positions, not to department heads."

"I don't think I am. I'm going to consult my union chairman."

"Be my guest, but I think Milt Levine is going to bear me out."

I rushed past him to the door.

"George," he called after me, "I really think you're putting too much emotion into this. Have a cup of coffee and simmer down. I don't want to give you any false hopes, but there's always the chance that Ms. Merman won't work out, in which case we can talk again. We really still want you with us."

"Because you know that Ms. Merman is really a phony."

"That's a harsh word to use about someone you don't even know."

I drew a deep breath, and yelled, "I hope that Rupert Murdoch buys out the *Globe!* And that he replaces you with an Australian who doesn't know Manhattan from Melbourne! And Washington from Wollongong!"

After that, I rushed out of his office. Out in the corridor I pressed repeatedly for the elevator and thought it would never come. Down on the third floor I hurried to the features department. Luckily, Milt Levine was at his desk instead of out interviewing the celebrity of the week, who will have been forgotten the following week unless the right PR with the right connections and unlimited expense account had been hired. I told Milt my story while he pulled at his eyebrows and looked sympathetic.

"Unfortunately, the son of a bitch is right about the union contract and that fucking loophole."

"There must be something we can do."

"Stick around a minute. I want to call up some of my spies and try to get the lowdown on this new dame."

I was too nervous to sit, and paced the floor until Sylvia Westin begged me to stop because she was trying to write a lead for her cooking column for gourmets and was afraid of getting one of her migraine headaches. She was still suffering from the Chinese take-out she ordered last night. The very polite young woman who took her order on the phone had assured her that the restaurant never used MSG in any of it dishes, including her own selection, Happy Family, which was number 55 on the menu.

It was just as well that I could not kill Warren along the road to his home. Where the undeveloped stretch used to be was now a shopping center, and a snow thrower and two men with shovels were clearing the sidewalk.

Milt Levine, after a few calls, had beckoned me back to his desk. "I think I have the picture now, and it's a pretty complicated one, so hold on to your jockstrap. Do you know Martha Taylor, the publisher's special assistant, the preferred title for a lobbyist who's back in the private sector after making all the right connections in Washington and City Hall?"

"Yes. I've found her a nice woman."

"She's also a nice aunt. She has a niece, Pat Merman, in Louisville, Kentucky, who recently busted up with her guy and went to pieces. Her mother, Martha's big sister, asked her if she could help little Patty latch on to something here in New York so that she can get away and forget. Martha said sure and asked her boss, Mr. Drew. Drew told her to go see Jack Warren, and so Warren had to come up with something for Pat since it was basically an accommodation for the publisher, in a manner of speaking. There were openings all over the joint, but Pat had never gone on to college or studied typing or computers or bookkeeping. Hence the mail room."

"He could have put her in as a regular mail clerk."

"I guess he thought that, despite women's lib, the physical labor involved would be too much for a female. Or maybe it wasn't a dignified-enough job for Martha's dear niece. Anyhow, that's the story I get, and I give it much more credence than I will to the campaign promises of the candidates in the next election."

"What can we do?"

Milt pulled at his eyebrows some more, and said that he could go through the motions of a grievance meeting, but he assured me from past experience that it wouldn't help. He advised me to hang in and pray that Patty was attractive enough to become the mistress of an editor or executive and was promoted out of the department. He went on: "When you spoke with her on the phone, did she sound sexy?"

"Not very."

"Maybe you should invest in a subscription to *Cosmopolitan* and send it to her anonymously."

I returned to the mail room so furious that I was afraid that my insides would burst.

"What took you so long?" Al said. "You're late for the edition. I got an angry call from Debra Austern of the drama department."

As I walked toward him, he saw my fist and expression and he back-stepped against the wardrobe.

"And you're another miserable fuck!" I yelled. "You knew about this all the time. We worked together thirty years. I saved your ass a thousand times. You've robbed the *Globe* blind with postage and petty cash and I never said anything. Frank Post saw you at Yonkers Raceway on the day you called up and said you were having a kidney stone attack and had to make an emergency appointment with your urologist."

He glanced over my shoulder at the door, and cried under breath, "I have no idea to what you're alluding. Watch out I don't sue you for slander and defamation of character."

I grabbed his shirt collar. "When did you ever have any character?"

"Let go! You're crushing my tie. It's a genuine Countess Mara from Saks Fifth Avenue."

"Fuck her."

"You're uncouth," he snarled. "You don't belong with civilized people. Frustration comes to everyone, and some things in life we have to take like a man. Ralph Waldo Emerson says—"

"Fuck Ralph Waldo Emerson."

I had him against the wardrobe and I wanted to beat his fat, ugly head till he fell, and then stomp him till he was dead. It took all of my self-control to refrain. I pushed him aside so that he went crashing into a desk, and then I yanked open the wardrobe and pulled out my jacket.

"I didn't give you permission to leave early today," he yelled. "I'm not yet gone from the premises that you can start goofing off. I hereby order you to go down for the edition, and you can be sure your insubordination will be brought to the attention of the proper quarters. If I didn't happen to be retiring in two weeks, I would fire you on the spot."

Fresh copies of his two original index cards still hung on the wardrobe door. I pulled them off and started to tear them up.

"Hey!" Al cried. "That's personal property of mine. You're acting just like a commie, which you probably are."

I finished tearing the cards, and threw them up in the air.

"I always knew you were a slob," Al said. "You never really had the right stuff. But all these years I tried to give you the benefit of the doubt. I should have fired you the first week."

"You should have," I said.

I turned and walked out of the mail room for the last time. In the doorway, I did not pause for a last, lingering, backward look. I think it would have killed me.

And now, in another minute, I was going to kill Jack Warren. I turned into Woodview Road and saw his house diagonally across the street. Early in his career he had bought it with an inheritance from his father. As he climbed the ladder of success at the *Globe,* he had seen fit to improve his property rather than move to another house or another area. It was now almost twice the size of my first view of it many years ago, with additional wings and a covered veranda instead of a few wooden steps and a small porch. The home improvements had been done at a deep discount or even on the cuff by supply companies that wished to continue to do business with the *Globe.* Or, for example, in the case of a certain popular restaurant chain, to avoid publication of a Health Department report about the filth in its kitchens. Covered with snow, it looked today like the all-American home in a Christmas card by Norman Rockwell. A teenager was shoveling snow on the sidewalk in front of the building just before his. Alice and some friends from church had joined the Tai Chi class at our local Jewish Community Center, and I performed Ms. Lippman's breathing exercise for total relaxation till the kid had finished and gone into his house. The one time I saw Ms. Lippman, at a Chanukah party at the center, she was far from relaxed as she complained about the nonmembers of her class who had appeared out of the blue and were devouring all the refreshments, especially the miniature Danish and rugelach, which were strictly kosher and far more expensive than the usual doughnuts from Entenmann's.

The kid having gone finally, I crossed the street and walked up the block. I turned my head aside as a van drove by. There was a pounding in my head, but I felt calm and in control.

Warren had parked his Olds at the curb. Pasted to its window was the green and yellow sticker that entitled him to park in the executive lot behind the Globe Building. Footsteps in the snow led from the car across the wide lawn to the entrance, and I stepped into those as I approached. From a policeman friend in my neighborhood, I had learned that the value of footprints and fancy detection was greatly exaggerated in the media and in fiction, and that the hot leads usually came from stoolies and from spouses and lovers who had been dumped for someone new and improved in the bedroom, hopefully, but I didn't want to take any chances in case my friend was wrong.

I glanced at my Timex. Setting the correct time for me when I bought it, the pleasant saleswoman at the Alexander's department store in the World Trade Center had said, "May it tick only happy hours for you."

"From your mouth to God's ear. How long do you think it'll last me?"

"Frankly speaking, what do you expect for $24.95 plus tax? A Rolex, maybe?"

"I read in the *Times* recently of a man who bought a phony, five-dollar Rolex from a panhandler on Park Row, and it's been keeping perfect time for almost three years."

"It's quite possible. Einstein said that time is relative, and so maybe are phony Rolex watches, some being better in relation to others."

It was now 4:32. I knew from my timetable that the next return train was at 5:02. After that came one at 5:40. I would aim for the earlier train. I didn't want to hang around in Bay Shore a minute longer than necessary. I was sorry I hadn't thought to ask Mr. Anthony for a silencer.

I wondered what Alice was doing at this moment. Probably, she was tidying up her desk. She was going to be disappointed and worried to come home and find neither me nor a steaming meat loaf. I was sorry now I hadn't called her from Penn Station to say I might be a little late. By this time, too, the cat would be famished. Lately, since my unemployment, I'd been giving Rocky a little snack at about three, and she had gotten used to it. She was as tough as Sylvester Stallone in the movie, and I had given her the name before learning her sex.

There was a Colonial-style knocker on Warren's door, but it was only an ornament and couldn't be raised. As I pressed the bell, I was glad that Alice had warned me to wear gloves that morning. What excuse could I give her for coming home late?

"Walking in the midtown area after an interview that didn't pan out, I ran into Stuart Kurtz, who years ago used to be in the drama department. He's now associated with Patty White. You remember Patty White the singer, don't you? She's planning a big comeback and may be in the market for a chauffeur-bodyguard and all-around helper. Kurtz took me out to see her on the Island where she's staying. She was pleased and seemed interested. I'm keeping my fingers crossed. And I'm very sorry you had to make dinner yourself after a hard day. We'll go out somewhere nice if I get the job with Patty White."

That would do nicely, I thought.

I heard footsteps finally. Then, without anyone asking who it was, which was unthinkable back in Brooklyn, the door was pulled wide open. The vestibule was dark and I could barely make out Warren for a few seconds. He could probably see me more clearly in the twilight. He had taken off his overcoat but was still wearing a suit jacket, which I myself never did at home except on holidays when company was coming.

He did not look surprised to see me. At least, he didn't open his mouth and gape. I could have been an expected visitor who had arrived after he had given up hope of my ever coming. Finally he nodded his head and made a weak smile.

"Why, it's good old George Mancuso."

"Good afternoon, Mr. Warren."

"Come on in, fella. Come on in before we freeze our dicks."

This was going to be easier than I had thought. I brushed off my hat and coat and stamped my feet before I stepped inside and said, "Sorry about your floor."

He closed the door and offered me his hand. "What's a wet floor between old friends? Anyhow, since Bernice saw fit to leave my bed and board, the housekeeping here isn't as fastidious as in days of yore. Once a week I have a girl in."

My stomach heaved. I hadn't expected a witness. "If she's here now, I wouldn't want to upset her by tracking the wet all over."

"No, I'm all alone now. Lately she's been coming on Monday."

Which meant that his body might not be discovered till six days later. Somehow I had to get him down to the basement. Years and years ago, while his kids were still young and living at home, I had heard him mention to Al that he had soundproofed the basement so that they could play their rock records there without disturbing him upstairs while he worked in his den. And more recently, while a granddaughter was staying with him, he had mentioned again that he was glad he had a soundproof basement where the kid could play her Michael Jackson tapes and suchlike deafening idols of hers.

Playing the perfect host, just as he used to play the perfect boss, he helped me off with my coat and hung it up in the slatted white wardrobe extending from the door to the archway. The wardrobe was full of wooden and plastic hangers, but it had only male garments, which hung close together at one end. It looked as if burglars had walked off with the rest of its contents.

"Well, well, George, and what brings you to this neck of the woods?"

"I happened to be in town to visit an elderly uncle,

and I remembered that you live here too, and so I thought I would pay my respects."

"That's certainly very thoughtful of you, George. But then, that's just the sort of thing you would do." He opened his mouth to say something else. But he just shook his head. "Let me take your portfolio."

"I think I'd rather hold on to it. I may forget it when I leave. My uncle gave me some letters he wanted me to mail from Brooklyn so that they'll arrive faster."

Warren gave a laugh as he put an arm on my shoulder and led me through the archway. "Good old George. Once a mail clerk, always a mail clerk."

I gave a laugh too, saying to myself, *That's what you think, buddy.*

"I think we'll be more comfortable in the den," he said, leading the way through the half-darkness. "This is certainly an unexpected pleasure. More and more lately I've been thinking of the old days at the *Globe*."

"We certainly go back a long way together, Mr. Warren."

"You can say that again. And after all these years of our association, I really think you should call me Jack."

"Thanks, Jack."

The name didn't sound right. I knew I would always think of him as Warren or Mr. Warren. When I thought of his body lying in the cemetery, I would think of Warren's body, not Jack's.

The den smelled of leather, and I thought of dead

animals. I definitely had to become a vegetarian one of these years. If Alice hadn't already prepared the meat loaf herself when I arrived home, I would suggest a nice cheese or vegetable omelet for dinner.

The drapes were drawn together, which suited my purpose, and in the darkness I could barely see Mr. Warren as he bent over a lamp upon a table. The light sprang out, but he continued at the switch until it clicked to a lesser brightness. I thought he was conserving energy like a good citizen.

And then he turned to me, and I was surprised by the change in his appearance. His face was bony, and the flesh hung loose from his throat as though it had been stretched. There were pouches under his eyes as if he hadn't slept in weeks, and there was also a red splotch on his brow. He looked like a caricature of his former self drawn by Steve Burnstein, the *Globe*'s editorial cartoonist. His hair, though, was even thicker than I remembered it, and had no gray at all that I could see. I assumed that, like more and more men these days, he was coloring it for business or social reasons.

His hand passed through the air from the sofa to the wing chair to the reclining chair. "Take a load off your feet while you tell me what you've been doing with yourself." He walked across the carpet to a cabinet upon which stood several huge and impressive trophies, probably for his golf and bowling. "What are you drinking these days?"

"Please don't bother," I said, thinking of fingerprints upon the glass.

"I insist that we have a drink together upon the occasion of this reunion."

"In that case I'll have a Hennessy," I said, not wishing to mix my drinks for the day though it was many hours since the bar and Cathy. I wondered how many other drinks the poor woman had had by now, and how many other men she had gone to bed with.

"I'll have to give you Martel."

"A Martel will be swell," I said. It was a nice rhyme for a jingle in a TV commercial, and I wondered if I might have a hidden talent for writing song lyrics.

While I sat down on the edge of the wing chair with the portfolio on my lap, Warren poured the brandy into huge snifter glasses such as William Powell and Ronald Colman used to offer to their ladies fair. He delivered my drink with more flair than my previous bartender that day. Sitting down on the sofa about two yards from me he said, "Here's to those good old days that are gone forever."

Sipping, I thought that he too would be gone forever, and in only a few minutes.

He set down his glass on a coffee table and folded his hands on his lap. "Now tell me what you've been doing with yourself since you left the old rag."

"I'm truly surprised to hear you, of all people, call the *Globe* a rag."

Warren gave an explosive laugh, and then, with a sly smile, he glanced to his left and right. "Since Meredith J. Drew is out of earshot, I think we can let our hair down and admit that the *Globe* is hardly the *Times* or the *News* or *Newsday* or even the *Post*. Anyhow, not so long ago I too severed my relationship with the *Globe*."

"I hadn't heard."

"I'd been planning to make the move for quite some time." He heaved a deep sigh, and then picked up his glass and swallowed the rest of his drink. "But enough about me. Tell me about yourself. What've you been doing since that regrettable day in my office?"

"As you know, when I had trouble finding a decent job right away, I applied for unemployment insurance."

Warren turned away from me. He arose with a groan and went to the cabinet with his glass.

I had not intended to apply for unemployment insurance, since I didn't consider myself legally entitled to it because I had left the *Globe* voluntarily and not been dismissed. But a friend who worked for the Democratic Party insisted that I had quite a good case for insurance, on the grounds that the *Globe* had made it so unpleasant for me that I was forced to quit for reasons of emotional health. This seemed to be the truth, in a way, and so I applied after all. Rejected at my local office, I asked for a hearing, and it was held a few weeks later at the World Trade Center. Sally Vincent, assistant to their house attorney, appeared for the *Globe*. She told the hearing judge that I was not considered worthy of promotion because I had assaulted Al Vann without cause, and she said that I quit my job because I had a macho mentality and refused to work under a woman. The judge, who happened to be a woman too, and a protégé of Congresswoman Bella Abzug, sided wholeheartedly with the *Globe*, and she ruled that I was not entitled to benefits. Also, she advised me to catch up on the lives and careers of Eleanor Roosevelt and Barbara Jordan. I would learn from them that men were no longer and would never again be the masters of all creation.

"A refill?" Warren asked.

I had hardly touched my first. I wanted my brain to be clear. I finished answering about my recent activity: "But then things improved, thank God, and I got a job with Con Edison, where I'm doing nicely with hope of a raise and a promotion."

"I'm glad things worked out for you. My mother used to say, 'God never closes a door without opening a window.'"

"So did mine," I said. But she never warned me that someone might sneak up behind me and push me out of the window.

He sipped his drink, then looked thoughtfully across the room at some framed writing that was probably a testimonial. He saw me glance at my watch.

"Stay awhile," he said, almost pleading. "I'm glad of your company. I don't remember my last visitor here."

"I was intending to catch the 5:02 back."

"The station's only a few minutes away. I'll drive you. Or, better, stay for dinner. I'm sure I can scrape up a little of this or that. Better still, I know of a pretty good seafood restaurant on Merrick Road."

"Thanks, Mr. Warren, but my wife is expecting me."

He pointed to a phone on a table near the window. "Give her a ring and tell her you've run into an old buddy."

"I wish I could, but tonight's our anniversary," I lied.

"I see. Well, that certainly comes first." He looked down at the finger upon which he used to wear his wedding ring. "Two Saturdays ago was my own anniversary, but I no longer had a wife to celebrate it with."

"Are you thinking of marrying again?"

He shook his head, and finished his brandy, and stared into the glass. "If you knew how funny that remark was...."

I thought he was about to tell me why he and his wife had divorced, and I was curious to know. The office gossip at the time had been that, despite his advanced years, he was making out with Jennifer Kiley, a secretary, and when he refused to appoint her his special assistant, she had accidentally on purpose mentioned the relationship to Phyllis Welles in the drama department, who was distantly related to his wife.

"I had always thought the old saying to be just romantic bullshit," he continued, "but I guess there may be a grain of truth in it. For every man there's really only one woman in the world. Along the way he may be tempted by other dames with better looks and personality and conversation, but...." He looked into his glass and seemed surprised it was empty.

I thought of Alice and myself. "I guess you're right."

"I know I'm right. And I found it out the hard way."

With a greater effort and deeper groan than before, he rose to his feet. He swayed a little. "This is the most I've had since Christmas and New Year's, and it seems to have gone to my head. I guess the old carcass ain't what it used to be. In fact, I know it ain't." He hesitated, and then said almost confidentially, "The doctor has told me to cut down."

"I guess we're all getting a little older," I said, and put a hand to my hair. I smiled. "But you still have all of yours, at least."

He looked at me, and snickered. "How about another drink? You're falling way behind. You'll never make a proper executive at the *Globe*."

"That's for sure."

He went to the cabinet for another drink, which he started to sip on his way back to the sofa. I hoped he wouldn't pass out before I could shoot him.

He changed his mind about sitting down, and walked over to the fireplace where he placed an arm upon the mantel like the men of distinction in the old ads for Calvert's rye. Any second now I was looking forward to changing him into a man of *ex*tinction.

"Did I just detect a note of bitterness in your last remark?" he asked.

I shook my head. "Why should there be bitterness between us? Why in the world?"

He turned out his hands in a gesture of incomprehension. "Why indeed? But people do have a way of misconstruing. I'm glad you're not one of those. In industry, and also in other fields of endeavor, an executive often has to do things...."

"Please don't bother to explain yourself. I'm sure you had reasons for doing what you did."

"I did. Believe me, I did. And I'm glad you're being a gentleman and taking such a positive attitude. Norman Vincent Peale would be proud of you, and send you an autographed copy of his book. I'm sorry now it was never in my small power to do more for you at the *Globe.*"

"I'm sure you did what you could, Jack. In fact, you did plenty."

He didn't pick up on my irony. Or pretended not to. "I did, I did," he said, with all the force and sincerity of Orson Welles, an actor trained for Shakespeare but forced in his decline to sell a non-gourmet wine in TV commercials.

Raising his glass to his mouth, he walked over to the window and parted the drapes and stared out. I seized this opportunity to pull a tissue from my pocket and wipe my glass. He turned abruptly and stared at me.

I explained: "I thought I saw a little ant or something in my glass."

"I hope you're not becoming a hypochondriac like Al Vann."

I had sat down without touching the leather wing chair, and now I arose without touching it either. "I wonder, while I'm here, if I could see your basement."

"My basement?" He threw a sharp look at me, and I thought that he was beginning to suspect my ulterior motive.

I made a bright and admiring smile. "My son is in the contracting business, and he's having a little trouble on one of his current jobs. I remember your once mentioning that your own basement is worthy of an article in *Better Homes and Gardens*."

A smile of pride lit up his face. "Of course. Sure. It'll be my pleasure. I designed it myself, and it's one of the few things I have left to show for my efforts of sixty-three years. Take along your drink."

"I think I've had enough for a while."

"Come to think of it, George, I can't recall ever having occasion to reprimand you for lack of sobriety on the job."

"No, you never did. But your colleague and pal, Sally Vincent, mentioned at my hearing for unemployment insurance that I had been drinking more and more on the job. And that I once threw up on the penthouse floor. She said it was lucky that Mr. Drew was not on the premises that day."

"That's news to me. I wonder where she picked up an idea like that."

"Maybe at the law school she attended."

He picked up his glass and gestured me to follow him. We walked through an untidy kitchen and came to a door that he opened and then reached beyond to flick a switch.

"Age before beauty," he said, motioning me to precede him down the stairs.

I suggested that he close the door behind him in order to conserve heat. He shrugged and complied. I walked slowly, in case I had to catch Warren, who was uncertain of his footing. If I had been walking behind him, I would just have to give him a little push and he would probably have fallen and broken his skull. On the other hand, they say that the inebriated survive accidents better than the sober.

"Do you keep in touch with Al Vann?" I asked to make conversation.

"Are you crazy? Who wants to keep in touch with such a miserable and neurotic creep? It's enough that I had to deal with him all those years at the paper."

"This comes as a surprise to me. If he was a miserable and neurotic creep, why was he kept on for so long? Maybe it's true what I sometimes heard, that he had a relationship with Mr. Drew's sister, and that they had met at a lecture at the Ethical Culture Society on Central Park West."

"That may have been a factor in the beginning, but once she died of that overdose of prescription drugs, Mr. Drew had no qualms about dumping Al. But I was able to convince him that power-hungry neurotics like Al are useful if not indispensable for keeping the troops in line. If you had attended business school, you'd have learned that the very first semester. Of course, it would have been presented in more academic terms and with quotes by Peter Drucker, author of *The Effective Executive*. I more or less remember one of them from my own class at Columbia: 'Effective leadership is not about being liked. It's defined by results.'"

"Speaking of leadership, have you heard how Pat Merman is running the mail room? I assume she lived up to your great expectations. You couldn't have been more proud of her if she were one of your own kids."

"I don't give a shit about the mail room anymore. The last I heard, two of the clerks had walked out on her after she changed their hours without notice and also wanted them to do personal favors for her as if she were a longtime executive and in a position to compensate them off the books and on the couch, as they say. One day she had to go down to the mezzanine floor to the circulation department. One of the truck drivers who happened to be there gave her a little goose like his daughter had experienced at the Fountain of Trevi in Rome, and the kid had enjoyed it because it indicated she was sexy and desirable. Pat did not enjoy it, maybe because she's gay, and she reported the guy to Martha Taylor in Drew's office. Acting on her own authority, Martha tried to have the guy disciplined, which almost caused a strike. Drew told her to lay off the truck drivers if she knew what was good for her. They were more indispensable to the operation than she and a dame in the mail room. All over the building, and for years and years, the drivers had been conducting a numbers operation that was connected to the Mafia, and once, when he, Drew, tried to close it down, they called a strike that lasted for six days until Drew surrendered and agreed to restrict his anti-gambling crusade to the verbiage of his reporters and columnists, and to his editorial writers, and to his eloquent speeches at the Better Business Bureau and the Harvard Club."

I looked with admiration at the basement: the bookcases, the TV and elaborate stereo, the tweed sofa and matching chair, the rocking horse in a corner, the dropped ceilings and paneling which probably created the soundproofing.

"Wow! It's certainly a production."

Warren wiped a finger across the top of the TV and stared at the smudge of dust. "Since nobody comes here anymore, my housekeeper doesn't clean with any regularity. Johnny is in Missouri and Claudia in Alaska. My granddaughter spent a little time here a while back, and nobody has been here since."

He turned around in place. He finished his drink in a single gulp and then flung his glass against the fireplace like aristocrats in foreign movies who don't have to do their own cleaning. "The hell with everybody and everything!" he screamed like the patients in my mother's hospital ward.

I looked at my watch. I could still make the 5:02 if I hurried. I unzipped my portfolio and inserted my hand.

Suddenly, Warren began to cry, a weeping that shook his whole body. With his head bent over, he turned around so that I couldn't see his face. I walked over to him. Under the bright fluorescent fixture, there seemed something peculiar about his hair, that the color was uniform and without a single gray hair, and I realized that, like Mr. Anthony at the Plaza that morning, he was wearing a wig. I wanted to laugh but couldn't.

His hand rose, but instead of stopping at his nostril it continued to his eye and rubbed it.

I removed my hand from the portfolio. For the time being. "Is there something I can do for you?" I said.

He clutched his throat as if he were choking. "There's nothing that anybody can do for me."

"Maybe call your minister or doctor?"

"Not since I was a kid have I believed in ministers or religion, which is mostly as big a racket as journalism. And it's too late for a doctor. I've seen all the doctors, including the best and most expensive of them all. I saw him in town only this afternoon. The fucken Yid had been away teaching in Israel, and I had to wait nearly a whole month for an appointment."

"As long as that," I said, looking surprised, and thinking of all the time that he, Jack Warren, had stolen from me.

"He's in the same building on Seventieth Street as Rhonda Shaw. Do you remember Rhonda from about ten years ago? She was Cy Raymond's secretary for a while. I told Cy she had to be a hooker on the side in order to live in such a swanky building, and it turned out I was right."

I remembered that the *Globe*, in its brief story about the police raid, had omitted the information that Rhonda was one of its employees. The *News* and the *Post*, on the other hand, mentioned her place of employment up front in their stories. Ordinarily, out of professional courtesy, they would not have mentioned her employer at all, but the three tabloids were having a circulation war at the time.

"I remember her," I said. "It's hard not to."

"I wish I'd been there to visit Rhonda instead of Dr. Zeigler."

"Sorry."

"Me too. But Rhonda herself was just thrilled and delighted. The stories turned out to be good publicity for her. A few issues later she was in *Playboy*, a few pages after Farrah Fawcett."

Warren raised his hand and pulled off his hair as he would have done with a hat. His scalp was bare except for stubble and a few wisps. I remembered his thick head of hair when I first came to work for the *Globe*.

"Chemotherapy!" he cried. "Everything I eat flows right out through my rear end. The doctors are surprised I can still get around. And so am I."

"Can I get you another drink?"

"Sure. If those first three don't kill me, maybe, hopefully, the next few will."

I was sorry now that I had suggested it. He pointed to a cupboard in a corner.

"Anything you find there will do," he said.

I found only gin and vodka, and poured a small amount of the vodka into one of the glasses. "Fill it up!" he demanded. "All the way!" His hand shook as he reached for it. "Thanks, buddy." After he had finished his drink, his hand still shook. He placed it on my shoulder. I looked away from his anguished eyes.

"Do you know what I believe, old pal?"

"What, Jack?"

"I believe that God or fate has sent you to me today."

Over his shoulder I saw my unzipped portfolio resting on the floor beside his liquor cupboard. I excused myself and went over to retrieve it.

Warren laughed. "Still worried about your uncle's letters, I bet. When I get to the Pearly Gates, which should be any month now, I'm going to recommend to St. Peter that you be put in charge of their mail room, if they have one."

"Please don't bother. I'm through with mail rooms. In heaven I intend to go in for playing the harp."

"That's very funny, George. I don't think I ever appreciated your sense of humor till this moment."

"Seriously, are a few months all you have?"

"It could even be only a few weeks." He put his hands over his face. "They wanted to cut up my liver but I said nothing doing. I've had it, George. After sixty-three years, I've had it. My health is gone. My wife is gone. My kids are thousands of miles away."

"Do they know about your condition?"

"Not the full extent of it. I don't want to bother them. If they came in for a visit, it would only be out of a sense of duty. We were never that close and I can't really blame them. When they were growing up, I paid more attention to the *Globe* than to them. I didn't come home till they were already in bed, and on weekends there was all that fucking golf and the cocktail parties."

I thought that my own children could never reproach me for preferring the *Globe,* golf, and cocktail parties to them. And I had gotten to know all their books of bedtime stories by heart. Both of them used to love, especially, *The Child's Garden of Verses* by Robert Louis Stevenson. I used to recite:

How do you like to go up in a swing,
Up in the air so blue?
Oh, I do think it is the pleasantest thing
Ever a child can do!
Up in the air and over the wall,

Till I can see so wide,
Rivers and trees and cattle and all
Over the countryside—
Till I look down on the garden green,
Down on the roof so brown—
Up in the air I go flying again,
Up in the air and down!

And at the end of the poem I would swing them up while they tried to touch the ceiling.

"I wish I had the guts to kill myself," Warren said.

"Don't talk like that."

"I think a lot about it. It's the thing I think most about except for death itself."

"Maybe there are other doctors you can see."

"There are no others," he said, extending his glass.

As I went to get him another vodka I glanced at my watch. The 5:02 had come and gone.

Warren's eyes were closed and he was holding his stomach in pain as I returned with his drink. He knocked the glass from my hand and grabbed my forearm.

"I'd like to ask a favor, though I probably don't deserve one from you."

"What is it?"

"Upstairs in my bedroom is a gun. It's on a closet shelf under some sweaters and mufflers. How about bringing it down and shooting me? And while you're there, you can pick out any sweater and muffler you like. In fact, take as many as you like. Some are pure cashmere that I picked up in Edinburgh and London. There's a white cardigan in which I used to play my best golf. I once told my wife I'd like to be buried in it. She thought it wouldn't be respectable for people in our position."

"You're kidding about the gun."

"I've never been more serious."

"I think you've had one too many."

"I've had just enough to make me see everything crystal clear. The doctor wanted me to go into the hospital today. He even offered to have his office assistant give me a lift to Sloan-Kettering, which was in the neighborhood, and he would probably have added only a hundred bucks to my bill for his kind service." He put a hand on my shoulder and stared into my eyes. His lips twisted into a smile. "What do you say, old buddy? How many years were we together?"

"Thirty at least."

"That long?" He shook his head. "Is it too much of a favor to ask after such a long relationship?"

"Would you like me to get in touch with your kids?"

"They can't do anything for me. If they were interested in their old man, they would visit or at least phone, and they don't."

"How about your wife?"

"I don't have a wife anymore. About six months ago I passed her in Rockefeller Center with her new hubby. To burn me up, she took his hand and smiled adoringly at him as if he looked like James Garner instead of being fat and almost bald and wearing a jacket that looked like it came from a thrift shop in Brooklyn. She'd like nothing better than to hear of my present condition."

"I can't believe that. Anyhow," I reminded him, "there are all your friends at the *Globe*. You used to have lunch with Roland Gelman all the time, and go out for drinks with Bob Wilson and Eugenia Ross."

My remark so infuriated him that he kicked his hairpiece across the floor. Somehow he lost his balance, and he would have fallen if I hadn't rushed forward to steady him.

"They stopped writing and phoning a long time ago. I received just a single lousy letter from Drew. It was extremely formal. He'd dictated it to his secretary while probably feeling her tits. That's the kind of bastard we worked for all these years. No gratitude for long devotion. We were just cogs in his machine. Cogs! Cogs!"

I shrugged to convey that there was nothing we could do about it now. I took another look at Jack Warren and decided there was nothing more I wanted to do here. I zipped up my portfolio.

"I guess I should leave now if I'm going to make the next train."

"I'm willing to pay you for the favor, George."

I ignored his remark and put the portfolio under my arm.

"What's the going price for a Mafia hitman these days? Whatever it is, I'll double it."

"I don't know anything about things like that."

"Don't kid me. You're Italian, aren't you? Naturally, I would leave a suicide note so there would be no question of your implication. My various doctors would testify that I was a dying man. My shrink, Dr. Julian Mariner of Madison Avenue, who studied Zen with Alan Watts in California, and is as crazy as any of his patients, would testify that I've been morose and depressed with an urge for suicide. What do you say, old pal?"

"I really have to go, Jack. Do you want me to help you up to your bedroom?"

"Haven't you ever, in all these years, wanted to get even with me, George? Here's your chance. And you'll be paid for it, and won't be punished."

"I don't want to get even with you."

"If you'll pardon my saying so, you're a fool to overlook this rare opportunity."

"I already know that I'm a fool compared to people like you."

"But you probably don't know how big a fool."

"Go ahead and tell me."

"When I hired you for the mail room, I had no intention of ever letting you advance to the city room. Al said you were his most efficient mail boy ever, and so why spoil a good thing?"

"I think I've known that a long time."

"I never spoke to Don Spector about you."

"I know that too."

"Once, Janet Beach in the drama department approached me and asked if I'd mind if she tried to get you into her department as an editorial assistant. She was impressed by your knowledge of movies and literature. And she once heard you humming a song by Schubert on the elevator."

"Go on."

"I told her you were incompetent, took days off, and had a drinking problem."

I hadn't known that one.

He jabbed a finger at my chest. "This Merman cunt is related to Martha Taylor and was an accommodation to her. She didn't know her ass from her elbow about mail rooms or anything else under the sun, and she never will." Warren paused for a deep breath, then said, "I've never been your friend. I've always had you down for a dumb Wop from Brooklyn and almost as much of an animal as a nigger or a spic. Don't you hate me?" His face was so close that I could smell his foul breath.

"It's certainly hard to *like* you, Jack."

"Get the gun. It's on a shelf in the master bedroom."

I looked at his bald head and sunken cheeks.

"Please get the fucken gun and shoot me!"

I shook my head. I wanted to tell him to go to hell, but I had an idea that he was already there. I shook my head again. I picked up his hairpiece by a thin strand, shook out the dust from the floor, and spread it on the television set where he wouldn't have to bend down for it. I had to get away from there.

I put out my hand to him. "Thanks for the drink and the hospitality. I have your number in my book, and maybe I'll phone you in a day or two. I hope something turns up for you. I'll think of you in church Sunday."

"Do that," he growled.

"I'll find my way out," I said.

While he walked over to the liquor cabinet, I turned toward the staircase. I was already halfway up the stairs when I remembered something. Walking down again, I took out Mark's Bible. At the cupboard, Warren turned to glare at me.

"Something you may care to look at," I said, and after showing him the gilt cross on the cover, I placed the Bible atop a wing chair.

Walking up the staircase and then across the foyer to the front door, I could hear him screaming at the top of his lungs. It reminded me of the night when I was a kid sitting on the end of a pier near Red Hook, Al Capone's old territory. There I heard a welsher being worked over by loan sharks.

I rushed all the way to the train station, which triggered an excruciating spasm in my left thigh. But I needn't have hurried, because the train was twenty minutes late, just like the commuter trains always being mentioned in the transit and weather reports on WCBS. It was as bad as the subway, and I was glad I wasn't a commuter. The train, when it arrived, was like a refrigerator. I sat shivering with my coat buttoned to the throat and my muffler over my ears.

At Babylon I changed to a train that was also late but had some heat at least. Passing Amityville, I thought of Patty White and wished her well in her comeback. I tried to read the Suzie Christopher book, but kept thinking of Jack Warren. And once again, I heard the man being killed by loan sharks on that pier:

"I'll pay you tomorrow. Honest. Honest to God."

"You had your chance, you dumb, fucken prick. Today was your deadline. We have our orders from the boss. Do you think he's a charity, maybe the Brooklyn branch of Christian Disaster Relief?"

"I swear to God, tell Vito that—"

There was a final long scream and then footsteps ran away over the squeaking planks. I lay on the pier about five minutes before daring to get up and leave.

After arriving at Penn Station, I called Alice and explained that I was following up a job lead out on the Island though I wasn't too hopeful about it.

"But, as they say, nothing ventured, nothing gained," I finished my story to her.

"As long as you're okay. Rocky was so famished that she clawed up the good chair in the living room. I got home just in time to rescue the drapes."

"I'm sorry. After all these years the chair isn't that

good anymore. When I start working again we'll look out for a sale at Macy's or wherever."

"I've made the meat loaf."

"You shouldn't have bothered. Hamburgers would have been great."

"Do you want spaghetti or rice?"

"Either will do."

"So I'll see you in about an hour, right?"

"Better make it a little longer. I still have that late job interview with Bernie Rhineland that I told you about."

"In case it's for a night job, I don't think I'm crazy about your working those hours. The doorman at Mr. Davis's building on Riverside Drive was recently knifed on his way home. Mr. Davis wishes him a speedy and complete recovery but hopes that he will be replaced by a younger and bigger man. Someone who knows judo and karate but won't want more money than the doorman now in the hospital."

"I've already made the appointment and don't want to appear irresponsible."

Huddled against the wall, sitting in dejection on a carton on the floor streaked with urine, there was one bag lady and derelict after another in the passageway to the subway. I wondered why this could happen in the supposedly richest and most democratic country on earth, and I wanted to send angry letters to Mayor Koch and Governor Carey and President Reagan. It would just be to let off steam, of course, because I knew that if those politicians and their power brokers really cared about the destitute, they would have done something for them by now, just as they had already helped their friends and supporters with favors and well-paying jobs.

I got off the subway at the West Fourth Street station and walked along Bleecker Street to Sal's Grotto, one of Big Nick's legit enterprises so that he could report business income on his tax returns. Snow was still falling, and if there had been a shoe store still open, I would have bought a pair of rubbers in a last-minute attempt to save my good Florsheims.

Inside the restaurant a stereo was playing a heart throbbing version of "Come Back to Sorrento" with a lot of mandolins. I knew that the two bruisers sitting at a table opposite the cashier were Big Nick's bodyguards. The younger of them, Jerry Cantelli, was the son of a former neighbor on Avenue U. He was always hungry as a kid, and I used to treat him to a Twinkie or Hostess cupcake. As we greeted each other, he raised his hand high so that I could notice his diamond ring and appreciate his success.

I gave the mâitre d' my name and told him I was a little early for my appointment with Big Nick. He stepped behind a partition painted with a view of the Bay of Naples, and then returned. Looking overjoyed at my good luck, he gestured me to follow him inside.

Sitting at a rear table with his back to the wall for security, Big Nick looked up from his antipasto and waved me forward with both hands as if I were bringing him a blessing from the Pope. He even paid me the courtesy of half-rising from his seat, or maybe he just wanted me to admire more of his blue pinstripe, which made him look like a WASP executive. With a snap of his fingers he summoned the waiter and ordered another wineglass.

"This is the best Pinot Noir in town," he said, pointing to the fancy label on his bottle. "Do you remember the cheap Chianti we used to chip in for at that place near McDonald Avenue? If we survived that poison, it was only because God was looking after us." He wiped his hands on a napkin and then crossed himself.

"I'm sorry if I'm a little early and interrupting your dinner."

"Sit down and get a load off your feet. Did you eat yet?" He snapped his fingers for the waiter again.

"No, but Alice is making her special meat loaf."

He laughed good-naturedly. "How can she make anything special out of meat loaf?"

"I guess she uses certain herbs and spices. Anyhow, we call it the special meat loaf. It's an old family recipe."

"I was just kidding. I'm sure it's terrific." With his hands folded across his chest, he smiled like a priest at a baptism while the waiter poured the wine, and then he and I picked up a glass. "To a long and happy association," he said, and took a sip. "How did it go with Anthony at the Plaza?"

"Fine. He's a very friendly gentleman."

"Too friendly sometimes. One of these days he's

going to shack up with the wrong guy's broad and wake up minus a pecker like Larry Belmonte. By the way, just between you and me, did he mention the names of his current broads to you?"

"No."

"Are you sure?"

"I swear."

"Not even Ginny Russo?"

I clapped a hand to my heart.

"Don't look so scared. I believe you. But one likes to know these things about associates. They can come in handy. 'Knowledge is power,' as they say. Ask anyone in politics or the business community."

"I don't think I can do it, Nick."

"Can't do what?"

I took a deep breath. "Work with you."

"You're crazy. You're talking like a meatball."

"Maybe."

"You're missing your last real opportunity in life. If you read the papers, you'll know that the corporations are exporting all the jobs to Mexico and China. 'Fuck the American worker,' they say."

"I know it. Still...."

"Any particular reason for your decision?"

"I'm too old to start out in something new."

"Is that the real reason?"

"I don't have the guts required for this line of work. I don't think I can kill a guy."

"That's dumb. Of course you can. There's nothing personal involved in the business. It's like a messenger making a delivery. Turn your head to the left. Do you see that little guy putting away the double order of stuffed clams?"

"I see him."

"Guess what's his score." When I shook my head, he raised five fingers of one hand and three of the other. "And yet he's the best family man I have the privilege to know. As regular as this here Cartier watch of mine, every Sunday come rain or shine, and irregardless of whether he's on a winning streak in golf, he's at early Mass at St. Patrick's on Mulberry Street with his wife and kids and grandkids."

I nodded to convey that I admired the man's devotion to God, his work, and his family. And then I told him, "I'd like to give you the gun back now."

"You're making a big mistake, my friend. Do you want to work in shit jobs for the rest of your life?" He slapped his chest and said, "Believe me, I'm talking to you as I would to my own brother, which is the way I've always felt about you and always will." He raised a hand to his eyes. "These contacts cost me plenty, but they're worth every penny. I remember the day years ago when I was wearing strong new eyeglasses for the first time and everything looked very different and I could hardly see, and those guys came into Sal's pizzeria and took a fancy to my Polaroid camera, a birthday present from my folks, and they tried to—"

I touched his sleeve. "Please. I don't want to hear that story again. I appreciate your kind offer, but I'm sure that something decent may yet turn up."

"You're fifty and ain't got no college degree, which means not that a guy is educated, necessarily, but that he's been exposed to formal education. That's what a college professor at Fordham once said on my favorite TV show, William Buckley's *Firing Line*. I certainly love that title. And the guy himself. For one thing, besides being a good Catholic, he remained loyal to Joe McCarthy and called him a crusader against communism, which also preaches atheism. Getting back, you don't know the first fucken thing about computers, which is what counts now."

I unzipped my portfolio.

Big Nick gave a deep sigh. And he shook his head. "I assure you, it's no sweat off my own balls. But I did have high hopes for you."

Looking away from him I said, "I appreciate everything. Believe me. I'm speaking from my heart."

He signaled for the waiter, who came over with a tray. "What can I give you now, boss?"

After the waiter had scooped up the antipasto plate and the bottles of oil and vinegar, Big Nick said to him, "And my poor dumb friend here has something for you."

As Big Nick pointed to a setting on a nearby table, I picked up the large white napkin and with it removed the gun from the portfolio on my lap. I wiped off my fingerprints before wrapping the gun and placing it on the waiter's tray.

Big Nick informed the waiter, "My friend will not be dining with me. He prefers to go home to his wife's meat loaf."

The waiter looked stunned. He shook his head and said, "I'm sorry to hear that. Truly, I think we offer the best food in town."

As I rose from the chair, Big Nick wished me luck, and so that my visit wouldn't be a complete waste of time, he insisted that I take home a cheese cake that had collapsed on top and was unsuitable for his patrons that evening, one of whom he had been tipped off, would be the restaurant critic of *Modern Gourmet,* who never revealed her identity till the end of her meal, if then. But his informant at the conglomerate that owned the magazine had supplied him with several pictures of this gourmet from hell. He clenched a hand as he added, "One thing in the world I hate is a sneak."

Afraid to offend him by refusing the cake, I accepted it with thanks, saying that cheese cake was my favorite dessert. To demonstrate that we were still pals and always would be, he offered to have Jerry, his bodyguard and chauffeur, take me home in his new Mercedes, but I told him that my doctor had recommended a lot of exercise for my arthritis and that the walk from the subway to home would do me good.

"In that case," he said in parting, "I'll send you the

name and address of the acupuncture guy who's been treating Father Dominick of Saint Theresa's. Last summer he couldn't kneel down without pain, but now he jogs around the reservoir in Central Park. Naturally, I offered him a bodyguard, which he refuses, but I did make him promise to jog only when there's other people around. God, this city has really become a jungle!"

Maybe it was the cheese cake that attracted the cat that came out of the alley on Avenue U near East Thirteenth Street. It tried to climb up my pants and coat, and when I pushed it off and walked away, it followed me crying all the way down the block, where I finally picked it up. It put its head on my shoulder and stared at me as if waiting for my answer to a question. But I didn't have an answer.

I crossed at the light and continued on my way home. The cat continued to stare at me wide-eyed. I didn't have an answer to human questions let alone cat questions.

Between my portfolio and the cat and the cheese cake, I couldn't open the door myself and had to ring the bell. Alice had washed her hair and was wearing a towel in a turban.

"What do you have there?"

"A lopsided cheese cake and a cat."

"Oy!" she said, having picked up some Yiddish at her Tai Chi class. "That's all we need in this house."

"The cheese cake was a special. The bakery made me an offer I couldn't refuse."

"And the cat?"

"It came free."

"So did Rocky, and now we have to buy a new chair."

"It was cold and hungry, and it likes me."

"Cats don't like anybody."

"Maybe they do, but have trouble expressing themselves."

The two cats didn't take to each other immediately, and began to snarl and hump their backs and claw at each other.

"I'm sure they'll learn to adjust," I told Alice.

"Sure, like the Jews and the Arabs, and the Serbs and Bosnians, and the English and Irish, and the whites and blacks."

"And let's not forget the rich and poor," I added.

"How was your day?"

"A day like other days. Job hunting."

"Anything special?"

"Nothing special."

"Something may turn up tomorrow. Change your clothes and wash up."

Alice's meat loaf was as delicious as usual, and I complimented her.

"For a change, I used my Aunt Maria's recipe. She was from Bologna."

"Ah!" I said, like Julia Child when her soufflé comes out just right.

We watched what was left of the evening's installment

of a rerun of *Winds of War* while we ate the delicious cheese cake with our coffee. I approved of Robert Mitchum's desire to protect America from the Nazis, but Alice thought him foolish to spend so much time traveling and meeting important officials that he neglected the emotional needs of his wife, Polly Bergen.

"What else can he do?" I asked. "He's a naval officer and has to follow orders."

"Is that what *you* would have done with *me,* leave me behind at home while you enjoyed the company of young blondes like this Victoria Tennant?"

"No, of course not."

Alice stared at me as if she doubted my sincerity. Fortunately, our new cat was playing with the electric cord of the TV, and I had an excuse to leave the table. While at the set, I suggested that we turn off *Winds of War* before it blew up a war in our own house. She agreed at once.

While doing the dishes, we discussed a name for the new cat, a male, and after several rejections on both sides, I suggested Warren.

"That's the name of your old boss, isn't it? I won't insult the cat with a name like that. I'm not a violent woman, but one of these days I'm going to visit the *Globe* and...."

"I'm sure God will punish him for his misdeeds."

"I certainly hope so."

He already has, I thought.

Already in our nightclothes, we returned to the living room and watched the last few minutes of a ballet program on Channel Thirteen. I remarked to Alice that it would be nice if the whole family could go to see *The Nutcracker* next Christmas. She said it would cost a small fortune. I replied that I would certainly be working by then.

On the eleven o'clock news on Channel Four, long after the usual reports on local murders and the economy, the newscaster paused a few seconds before giving the next story, and his hand rose to his chin. He happened to be Dave Rooney, a former *Globe* reporter who had resigned in a fury after his longtime beat was given to a new reporter who was a protégé of the managing editor, who also wrote a weekly column on religion. In revenge, Dave mentioned them prominently in a *New York* article that praised the cultural contributions of the gay community to the city. Both the editor and his protégé were immediately forced out of the closet, and eventually out of their jobs by Mr. Drew, who was personally participating in the renewal of a lucrative advertising contract with a hotel chain owned by a top official of the Knights of Columbus.

Dave resumed: "Here's some breaking news. John F. Warren, a top executive of *The New York Globe* for many years, died apparently by his own hand late this afternoon at his showplace home in Bay Shore, Long Island."

Alice turned to me on the sofa. "It's your old boss. We were just talking about him. Isn't that a coincidence?"

"Certainly is."

"The body was discovered by the police, after a 911 call from Edward Hobson, a neighbor across the street, and also head of the Woodview Avenue Block Watchers Association. Preparatory to shoveling snow, Mr. Hobson looked out of his window and saw a suspicious-looking stranger emerge from the Warren home. He felt uneasy, and finally he crossed the street to investigate into what he thought might be the latest in a series of robberies in the affluent, upper middle class neighborhood, famous in recent years as the birthplace of three-time Grammy winner Lady Fruitcake, formerly lead singer of The Meltdowns. Suddenly he heard a gunshot from the upper floor. The police, when they arrived, discovered Warren dead in the bedroom. Nearby on the floor was a .32 caliber automatic. Sergeant Andrew Dressler of the Bay Shore police suspects no foul play, and he believes that the suspicious stranger, since he carried a portfolio, was probably either a salesman or one of the evangelists who have been visiting the area in recent weeks. The sergeant's father, Jerry Dressler, former center of the fabled Massapequa Marauders of yesteryear, confirms the presence of an evangelist in town this afternoon. Mr. Dressler added. 'And if he wasn't really an evangelist, he certain behaved to me like a Good Samaritan.' Reached at his town house on East Sixty-ninth Street in Manhattan, *Globe* publisher Meredith F. Drew told a Channel Four reporter: 'Jack Warren is going to be sorely missed, but his record of accomplishment will be an inspiration for a long time to come. His recent poor health has been a matter of concern to his many friends at the *Globe*. I'm told that the police found a Bible on his bed. He was always a religious man, and I'm sure that his last moments were spent in prayer. He'll be in the hearts, and minds, and the prayers of us all.'"

After several commercials for prescription drugs that would cure diseases I had never heard of, Rooney began to report about the mysterious disappearance of bats from their caves in Kentucky. At that point, Alice and I agreed that it was time to turn off the television and get ready for bed. We agreed also that we would soon be getting junk mail from groups dedicated to saving the bats in Kentucky and all over the world, especially the ones in Transylvania, where they might be transformations of Count Dracula and his fellow vampires.

The cats seemed to be getting used to each other. From opposite ends of the foyer they were merely hissing and lashing their tails. If the Buddhists and Hindus were right about reincarnation, the cats would in a thousand or a million years be reborn as humans, when they would have access to our own forms of interaction.

I turned off the lamp on my night table. Lying beside me, holding her rosary, Alice was saying her prayers, which often took as long as a whole Mass in church. Earlier in our marriage I used to think her a little silly to pray so long. Now I had grown to learn that people can't pray long enough and hard enough. New York and the world, though wonderful and beautiful, were mysterious and frightening places. People could be cruel, and killed with words if not with guns. I myself had wanted to kill Warren, and if I *had* killed him, the cops would have picked me up at the railroad station before the train came.

Under the covers, so that Alice wouldn't suspect anything, I placed my hands together and began to pray at bedtime for the first time since I was a kid and my mother would force me to under threat of eternal damnation.

I prayed for Alice and the kids and myself, and that my adultery would be forgiven.

I prayed for Cathy, and hoped that she would get together again with Frederick. Or meet a worthy bachelor who could support her drinking habit. Or, better, get her to join Alcoholics Anonymous.

I prayed for Mark, who really didn't need my prayer.

My eyes watered and I sniffled as I prayed for friends at the *Globe* who had passed on.

"Are you okay, George?"

"Just my nose. All the running around today."

"Do you want the Afrin?"

"No, thanks."

"Sure? It's a fresh bottle. I had to throw away the old one, which expired over a year ago."

"I'm sure."

"Okay, but don't say I didn't warn you."

I prayed that Patty White's voice and boobs would see her through to a successful comeback. As Stuart Kurtz had requested of me, I would call her in the morning and try to give her the boost she needed. Maybe she was in the market for a chauffeur-bodyguard, in which case I would exaggerate a little and tell her that I had once worked in that capacity for Larry Belmonte. But then how would I explain away the fact that he was killed in Vegas? Before calling her, I would have to study the Suzy Christopher book on effective conversation.

Last, seeing him again before me on the street, and on the bus and train, and in his den, and especially in his basement as he pulled off his wig, I prayed for Jack Warren.

If you enjoyed this book—and I hope that you did—please consider posting a review at Amazon.com and www.goodreads.com. Thank you.

Hy Brett

BOOK CLUB DISCUSSION QUESTIONS

1. *The Hitman of Avenue U* is about George Mancuso, a workingman who is searching for justice in a world that has grown more and more alien to him. After spending thirty years of his life working for the New York *Globe,* he suddenly finds himself unemployed and unable to find another job. Can you identify with George and understand the frustration and despair he feels? Have you ever been, or do you know anyone who has been, in George's situation?

2. The story takes place on a cold day in 1981, soon after Ronald Reagan was sworn in as president, promising to bring the country out of its economic malaise. Do you remember those times or know anyone who lived through them? Did you find that the description of

them in George's story reminded you of times you have lived through?

3. Desperate after his long and futile search, George reluctantly decides to accept the offer of his childhood friend and now Mafia boss, Big Nick Lombardi, and become one of his hitmen. Big Nick says that George's age and unassuming appearance give him the perfect cover. Can you understand why George agrees to work for Big Nick?

4. The book follows George through the day that he picks out the gun he will be using in his new trade. Just having it with him gives him a confidence he hasn't felt for years. Have you ever had something that gave you confidence when you were down? What was it? And do you still rely on it?

5. As the day passes, we learn more about George, his early years, his years on his job, his hopes and dreams. Have you shared any of his experiences? Were you moved by them?

6. We also learn about George's wife, Alice. We discover how they met and what their life together is like. What do you think of their marriage? How do you feel about Alice?

7. The first adventure George has after picking up the gun is to be the victim of a confidence scam. Were you surprised by how he got out of it? Have you ever been approached by people like that? How did you react?

8. Despite the fact that he has the gun and is scheduled to be sworn into Nick's "family" that evening, George continues to look for a legitimate job. How did you feel about the way employers reacted to his phone calls?

9. What did you think of George's reaction when the bar he drops into is suddenly robbed by a gunman? Did it surprise you? Why or why not?

10. In the bar, George meets Cathy, an attractive woman who is also down on her luck. When she asks him to see her home, he is reluctant to do so but is too inexperienced to know how to get out of it. How do you feel about what followed?

11. Later in the day, George spots his nemesis, Jack Warren, the executive who kept George back all those years and is responsible for the dire situation George is in now. George begins to follow him, determined to kill him. As George follows Warren, we learn a great deal more about their relationship, and

also about the corporate workings and underbelly of a New York City tabloid. Did any of the revelations surprise you? What have your experiences been in the corporate world?

12. Along the way, as he follows Warren, George meets an Evangelist, a songwriter, and a blind man. What does his interaction with these people tell you about George?

13. When George and Warren are at last face-to-face in Warren's home, did you expect Warren to treat George the way he did? Why or why not?

14. What do you think of the way George gets his revenge?

15. How do you feel about George's meeting with Big Nick, and the way George's momentous day ends?

www.ingramcontent.com/pod-product-compliance
Lightning Source LLC
Chambersburg PA
CBHW031234120726
47905CB00002B/588